T0072537

POM Quest Tales

Money & Power vs. Unconditional Love

Jerry McCallson

BALBOA.PRESS

A DIVISION OF HAY HOUSE

Copyright © 2021 Jerry McCallson.

All rights reserved. No part of this book may be used or reproduced by any means, graphic, electronic, or mechanical, including photocopying, recording, taping or by any information storage retrieval system without the written permission of the author except in the case of brief quotations embodied in critical articles and reviews.

Balboa Press books may be ordered through booksellers or by contacting:

Balboa Press
A Division of Hay House
1663 Liberty Drive
Bloomington, IN 47403
www.balboapress.com
844-682-1282

Because of the dynamic nature of the Internet, any web addresses or links contained in this book may have changed since publication and may no longer be valid. The views expressed in this work are solely those of the author and do not necessarily reflect the views of the publisher, and the publisher hereby disclaims any responsibility for them.

The author of this book does not dispense medical advice or prescribe the use of any technique as a form of treatment for physical, emotional, or medical problems without the advice of a physician, either directly or indirectly. The intent of the author is only to offer information of a general nature to help you in your quest for emotional and spiritual well-being. In the event you use any of the information in this book for yourself, which is your constitutional right, the author and the publisher assume no responsibility for your actions.

Any people depicted in stock imagery provided by Getty Images are models, and such images are being used for illustrative purposes only. Certain stock imagery © Getty Images.

Print information available on the last page.

ISBN: 978-1-9822-7444-3 (sc)
ISBN: 978-1-9822-7445-0 (e)

Balboa Press rev. date: 10/28/2021

Contents

Van Muessen

Farris Hamley

by
Jerry McCallson

Prologue

Through the ages, there have been three evil problems cursing man: Sin, suffering, and death...

This is a story, or should I say, many stories, that all connected to one person – Farris Hamley.

The story begins with Farris's hateful grandfather, Willard Hamley. Willard's son, Clarence, continued the sin, suffering, and death. With the birth of Clarence's son, Farris, was the cycle going to continue? Was this man cursed by horrid behavior of his family's history? Maybe, just maybe, there was a new beginning on the horizon.

With his wife gone, Farris redefined his love. He now focused on the LOVE OF MANKIND. He tried to use his billions to help people in need. Not so fast, Farris! The L.A. District Attorney was determined of his corruption and was determined to put Farris behind bars for the murder of his wife. Yes, D.A. Hawkins made Farris his personal career project. This obsession affected Hawkin's home life. How could this mess get resolved? Was this Farris HAMLEY hated and despised without just cause? You decide!

The Making of a Monster

Hamley Farm - Wickers Wood, Missouri
1930

"Go tell Aunt Rhody, go tell Aunt Rhody, go tell Aunt Rhody, the old gray goose is dead," Clovis sang as he entered the kitchen from the back door.

"Clovis? Is that you?" Lusinda, his mother, said in a loud voice.

"Yes, it is me, mother," Clovis responded.

If the truth were known, it was this song and the color of their shirts that Lusinda used to identify her sons. Clovis had an identical twin brother named Clarence. Lusinda always made Clarence wear bright colored shirts; bright blues, greens, and yellows. Clovis had to wear dark blues, greens, and browns. Lusinda made it a point to control their wardrobes and much, much more. Today, Lusinda turned to her husband, Willard, in the living room and made a crass remark.

"Lately, Clovis has been singing that God-awful song. I wish that he would sing something a little more cheerful. What in the world is that kid thinking about these days?" Lusinda said to Willard.

"Lusinda, you don't think that he heard us talking in the living room yesterday, do you?" Willard asked.

"I don't think so. Nobody was in the house at that time," Lusinda replied.

Little did Lusinda and Willard know that there were shoe prints in the mud, outside of the living room window. The window was open about halfway and outside the window and on the ground, there were shoe prints about size 11. Clovis wore a size 11. Clarence wore a size 9.

Oh, that window, that bay for the enlightenment and evil on display. That dark pale precursor of what was about to be was showing its face. Willard and Lusinda's conversation at this window would become a super-stressor for Clovis.

"I think that we are okay. It is as you said – the house was empty. Thank God he didn't hear me say that Clarence was my favorite son. I have enough problems just being the pastor of the Sacred Heart Church.I don't need one more problem from some idiot son that can't behave. I wish that he would just snap out of it," Willard said.

"Keep your voice down, Willard. Sometimes the truth can cause problems – problems we don't need," Lusinda said to Willard.

"Oh, alright! He's still outside in the back yard. He can't hear us talk," Willard assured Lusinda.

"Willard, half the time, I think that boy is daydreaming. When is he going to snap out of it?" Lusinda said. "Willard, this year I think that we should get Clarence a pet dog for his 14th birthday. He has always wanted one for years. Let's do it!" Lusinda said.

"And Clovis, well, I think that he would be happy with some new work gloves for chopping wood. Our kindling box is always empty," Willard said.

"That's a great idea, maybe if he is busy, busy, busy, he will stay out of trouble," Lusinda said as she headed for the bathroom. Once she was inside, the house phone rang.

"Hello! This is Willard," he answered.

"Hello, Willard. This is Darla. You remember me? We met last summer on Myrtle Beach, South Carolina. I just wanted to tell you that it's a boy," Darla said.

"What do you mean by that... It's a boy!" he said in a loud voice.

"Oh, how quick they forget. You don't remember that we made love on the beach by the palm tree?"

Willard paused, thinking hard. "What is it that you want?" he asked the voice on the phone. "Money?"

"Relax, you're getting yourself too worked up. Your secret is safe with me. If I told my husband, he would kill us both. I just thought that you should know. I gave him your name as a middle name," Darla Henry said.

Soon, Lusinda came back from the bathroom.

"Who was that on the phone?" she asked.

"Oh, it was just a wrong number!" Willard said.

Little did Lusinda and Willard know that there were fresh footprints outside of the living room window. Clovis had heard the entire conversation. On his way back to the kitchen door, Clovis whispered to himself a few choice words.

"Oooh, snap out of it. Oooh, if you both only knew. I can snap if that's what you want. Oooh, idiot son, you say..." Clovis said.

Clovis came into the house through the kitchen door and stopped to remove his muddied shoes. He placed them into the shoe box and went into his bedroom and flopped onto his bed. As he stared at the ceiling, he whispered to himself, "someday."

It was that overheard conversation at the living room window, yes, the window, that became the birthplace of his lifelong torment and pain.

There had been too many times, Clovis had to put up with these thoughtless verbal assaults from Lusinda and Willard. In Clovis's mind, he thought that there would be some escape down at the old mill pond, but that too, became just another place for torment – a torment that was exacted by his favored brother, Clarence.

The mill pond, that is where Clarence and Clovis played after school. The mill pond was about 400 yards down the slope from the back of the house. At this mill pond there was a ridge hanging over a rounded rock from where Clarence would leap into the water below. The jump was about twenty-five feet. Both of them called it The Jump Rock. It was too bad that Clovis was afraid of heights and water. All he could do was to wade through the pond as a spectator watching Clarence, who boldly made the leap.

Clarence used his brother's fear as an opportunity to tease him.

"Oh, come on, chicken foot! Make a jump! Don't be a wimp. Grow a spine." Clarence would say. Such bullying talk continued through the years. If it wasn't Lusinda and Willard, it would be Clarence this, Clarence that. Oooooh, life was oh so good for their favorite son, Clarence. How much more could he take? Clovis had withdrawn into a silent rage.

Last night at the supper table, Lusinda chastised Clovis.

"Clovis! Sit up straight in your chair like Clarence. Stop shoveling food into your mouth. Watch Clarence. He eats like a gentleman."

Just then, Clovis reached for a dinner roll, grabbing two. Lusinda reached over and slapped his hand.

"Clovis, save some for Clarence," she yelled. Soon

afterwards, Clarence reached out and grabbed two rolls. Nothing was said. Lusinda just smiled.

Saturday came and went. Clarence got his 14th birthday present – a dog that he had always wanted. Clovis got a pair of work gloves that he never wanted.

The following day, while Clarence and Clovis were at school, Willard came back from a carpenter's house with a doghouse. It needed to be painted. When Clarence and Clovis came home from school, Lusinda called them both into the kitchen.

"Coming, mother!" Clarence yelled back.

"Clarence, Clovis, while you were at school today your father picked up a doghouse for your dog, Jake. Clovis, I want you to paint it for Clarence. Clarence, tell Clovis what color he should paint it," Lusinda said.

"I want the color to be brown," Clarence responded with a smirk.

"Brown it is. You heard him, Clovis," Lusinda said with a firm voice.

"But what if it rains tomorrow?" asked Clovis.

"Rain? That shouldn't be a problem. Just pull the doghouse into the shed and paint it. Is that clear?" Lusinda asserted.

"But what if it doesn't fit through the door?" Clovis said.

"Just do it. Understand?" Lusinda shouted.

"Yes, mother," Clovis said.

"There is one more thing. While I'm at the doctor's office tomorrow, Jake is not allowed to come into my nice clean house. Is that clear?"

The following day came quickly. Lusinda gave the

boys their instructions one more time as they left for school.

"Now, I'll be back at about five o'clock. Make sure you both do as I said," Lusinda said.

At three-forty, the school bus dropped Clarence and Clovis off. In about an hour it started to rain. Clarence looked out the kitchen window. He could not see Jake in the yard. Suddenly, they both heard Jake whining at the back door. Clarence opened the door and Jake ran right past the both of them and straight into the living room. Jake left a trail of muddy footprints throughout the house. Suddenly there was another crash. Jake had knocked over an heirloom lamp of Willard's, smashing it onto the floor. If that wasn't enough, he slammed into an end table and broke a family picture. Soon, Lusinda came back from the doctor's office. As she walked into the house from the back door, she followed the trail of muddy footprints of Jake. These led straight into the living room. Once there, she saw a mess of broken glass on the floor.

"Clarence, come in here right now," Lusinda yelled. Clarence came right away.

"What happened here? Explain yourself," she demanded.

"I don't know anything about that. I was studying in my room. When I came out, I saw Clovis and Jake over by the table. I just went back into my room to do a paper for school," Clarence said.

"Oh, I see! I get the picture. Clovis! Once again, it looks like you need a little attitude adjustment. That's all Clarence. You can go back and finish your studies," Lusinda said.

Clarence went back into his room.

Lusinda cleaned up the mess and waited for Willard to come home. As soon as Willard came home, Lusinda told him about the dog episode and the damages. Willard stared at Clovis and then he walked over to the phonograph. He called Lusinda over and handed her a record – *Beautiful Dreamer* by Stephen Foster, which featured a female vocalist with a pleasant voice.

"Lusinda, now play it good and loud, if you know what I mean," Willard said. Willard approached Clovis and ordered him into his bedroom. Willard came into the room behind him and slammed the door.

"Clovis, now pull up your shirt and lean over your bed." As soon as the music started, Willard pulled out his belt and started to whip Clovis on his back. Willard gave Clovis four big whacks. On the third, he drew blood from Clovis' back. As he proceeded to whip Clovis, he repeated his usual verbal assault.

"Why, why, why, can't you be more like Clarence? Just so you know, this was all for your own good. Now see what you did! You got blood all over my nice new belt." Willard wiped the blood off with Clovis' shirt and left the room as the music was still playing. Willard then walked over to Lusinda and praised her.

"Thank you, Lusinda, for playing that record nice and loud. I didn't want to let Clarence suffer the noise," Willard said.

Clovis never made so much as a scream while he was being beaten. He just laid there on his bed, face down, and stared at the floor. Soon he started to sing his favorite tune.

"Go tell Aunt Rhody, go tell Aunt Rhody, go tell Aunt Rhody that the old gray goose is dead."

One week later, Clovis decided to take Jake for a short walk. Within five minutes, there they were leaving the woodshed. Clovis had stopped there to pick up a shovel. Soon they both arrived down at the old mill pond. In an instant, Clovis struck Jake in the head three times, killing him. This all occurred while Clarence was playing softball at a park near school, it was game day.

After Clovis finished his terrible deed, he slowly walked up the hill toward the house. As he was walking, he began his song, "Go tell Aunt Rhody, go tell Aunt Rhody. . ." he sang. Once Clovis reached the house, he noticed that Clarence was back from his softball game. It got rained out. Clarence stood in front of the kitchen window and voiced a concern.

"Clovis, have you seen Jake? Just look at it outside. It's starting to rain. Where could he be?" Clarence said.

"Oh, don't worry. If he gets caught out in a rainstorm, it will teach him a good lesson. You know, it's all for his own good," Clovis said with a smirk.

Days went by and there was no Jake to be found.

"What do you think happened to Jake?" Clarence asked Clovis one day out in the yard.

"Oh, he probably ran off with some other dogs. They like to be with their own kind, you know," Clovis assured Clarence. Soon the missing-Jake-problem became a mystery with no good answers. Clarence seemed to agonize over Jake's absence. That was perfectly fine with Clovis. For the time being, Clovis embraced a quiet contentment, but for how long? Only Clovis knew.

The Gloves

One day, Lusinda was looking at the wood box, it was empty. She needed some kindling for the wood stove in the kitchen.

"Clarence, I want you to fill up the wood box. Clovis, you go with him and give him some help," she said.

Clovis knew what that meant. Anytime Clarence was given a job, Clovis knew that all of the work would be his and his alone. It didn't take very long to break Clovis. His peace of mind would soon turn to thoughts of rage. Lusinda looked out the kitchen window screen and yelled at Clovis.

"Use those gloves we bought you. It is a waste of good money if you don't. You'd better find them or else," Lusinda said.

"I misplaced them somewhere in the house," Clovis yelled back. Clovis knew exactly where they were. He decided to use them for a special event.

Clarence began chopping some wood when suddenly he got a sliver from the axe handle. Clovis had to, as expected, come over and finish the job. Once done, Clarence came back into the house carrying the bundle of chopped kindling.

"That's a good boy... Clovis, look what nice even pieces your brother has chopped. Now that's the way to do a good job! Good job, Clarence!" Lusinda affirmed with an affectionate voice.

Clovis just stood there behind Clarence and went into a hot mental burn. Everything was now back to normal. Another win for Clarence and a loss for Clovis. Clovis had done most of the work.

Clovis went into his bedroom and slammed the door. On the backside of the door was a door mirror. Clovis just stood there and looked into his own eyes and began to mock his mother.

"Oooooh, you'd better find those gloves! Ooooooh, you'd better find those gloves, or else," he said to himself. In the other room, he heard Clarence give out a yell. Lusinda was probing his hand for a wood sliver. Clarence's painful yell gave a sense of pleasure to Clovis. His face broke into a half smile each time he heard Clarence yell from Lusinda's probe. Once again, Clovis mocked Lusinda.

"Ooooh, you'd better find those gloves, or else... Ooooh, I will, but not today," he whispered.

It was about one week after Jake's disappearance and the wood chopping event when Clarence came home from school. In his hand was a book report. He had written a paper on Yellowstone Park. Across the top of the paper was an A.

"What's this?" Lusinda asked as Clarence placed it in her hand.

"This is the homework I was working on when Jake messed up the house," Clarence said.

"Let me see, oh, what a great job you did on that paper. You certainly turned out to be our pride and joy. Just wait until I show your father," his mother said.

Once again, Clovis got an unwanted dose of how wonderful it is to be Clarence. Clovis then went to his room and came back with one if his papers. It only had a B+ at the top of the page.

"Oh, that's nice Clovis. Go and check the wood box. Make sure it is full," Lusinda remarked.

That evening after supper, Lusinda showed Willard the A paper, but not Clovis's academic achievement. The very next day, Clovis took out the kitchen trash and tossed it into the main bin. But something caught his eye. It was his paper all covered with spaghetti sauce. Lusinda had thrown it out. The following morning at breakfast, Lusinda made an announcement.

"Tonight, your father is going to take us all out for supper at Floyd's Restaurant because Clarence got an A paper from school," Lusinda said.

When their supper was finished, Willard went up to the owner to pay the check.

"I guess it is time to pay the check," Floyd said in a loud voice. Floyd had a loud deep voice. He used this same sentence on every customer for the last twenty years. Those words – *it is time to pay the check* – stuck in Clovis's mind.

Oh, Clovis thought with a long pause, *it is time to pay the check.*

"Some day, but not today," he whispered.

Willard's New Car

Fall 1932

In the fall of 1932, a neighbor of Willard's had purchased a new 1932 Ford Coup for $490. That neighbor had overspent his earned income. His current bills were exceeding his ability to pay. Willard stepped into rescue. He offered to buy the man's car for $300 cash. The deal was finalized and then Willard came home with the new car.

This car became the second most important thing in Willard's life behind his favorite son, Clarence. What was fortunate for Willard became unfortunate for Clovis, for it was now his job to keep it all waxed up and beautiful.

One Saturday afternoon in September, a friend of Willard's named Cy Vickers came over to the house to see Willard. Cy's visit was quite simple. He just wanted to show Willard the new paint job he did on his house, so Cy picked up Willard and drove him back.

While Willard was gone, Clarence decided that he wanted to take a short spin in the new 1932 car.

"Say, Clovis, let's take dad's Ford for a little spin. Nobody is here. Nobody will ever know," Clarence said.

"No! I don't think that is such a good idea," Clovis said with a firm voice.

"On, come on chicken foot. Grow a spine. You are afraid of everything," Clarence said. As always, the pressure was on. Clarence prodded Clovis. Soon Clovis gave in and got into the car. Soon they were speeding down the gravel road. Clarence was driving too fast.

First, Clarence would drive down about a half a mile, then he stopped the car after he turned around. Now Clarence decided that Clovis was going to do the same.

"Come on Clovis, get behind the wheel. Let's see what you can do!" Clarence said. Clovis got behind the wheel and began to drive very slowly. Clarence quickly became bored with the slow driving, so he stuck his foot over the top of Clovis's foot on the accelerator.

"Clovis, you drive a car like an old lady. You've got no zest for life. Come on, live a little," Clarence said.

The harder Clarence pressed down on Clovis's foot, the more out of control the car became. They were speeding on loose gravel. Suddenly, the car hit a farmer's mailbox. The crash damaged Willard's right fender.

In surreal fashion, the county sheriff happened to drive by after the accident. There he was. It was Clovis who was behind the wheel, but Clarence caused the accident. Of course, the sheriff noted in his report that Clovis was the driver, and so he was the one who got the citation.

"So, aren't you Parson Hamley's kid?" the sheriff asked.

"Yes, that I am," Clovis responded.

"Well, I'm sorry, I still have to give you a citation. You know, it is for your own good," the sheriff said.

That evening, the sheriff came by the house to speak with Willard about the accident. Willard was completely unaware of all the damages to the car and the mailbox.

After the sheriff left the house, Willard called Clovis into the living room. Willard stared at Clovis with angry eyes.

"Lusinda, the phonograph!" Willard said.

Lusinda started to play an old familiar song – *Beautiful Dreamer.*

"Now get yourself into your bedroom and assume the usual position over the bed," he demanded.

"It wasn't my fault! It wasn't my fault," Clovis pleaded.

"Shut up and remove your shirt," Willard yelled out. Clovis complied.

Just when the music on the phonograph got louder, Willard removed his belt and began with his assault. Some familiar words came out of his mouth as he whipped Clovis.

"This is all your fault. This is for your own good. Why can't you be more like your brother, Clarence?" Once again, Clovis took the whipping without a whimper. The next day, Clovis remained silent. He knew that telling the real story about the accident would not change a thing. Clarence would always get a free pass for his bad behavior.

Being despised and rejected without just cause, was now taking a real toll on Clovis. Life was becoming unbearable. How much more could he take? Clovis pondered that question when he was alone in his bedroom. He went over to the mirror on the backside of his bedroom door and just stared into his reflection, then began to whisper.

"Ohhhh, can't you be like your brother? Ohhhh, why can't you be Clarence? Ohhhh, you'd better find those gloves, or else... Ohhhh, it's time to pay the check," Clovis said.

The very next day as Clarence came out of his bedroom, there was Clovis standing there and staring into space. Suddenly, Clovis turned his face and stared right into Clarence's eyes. Clovis uttered, "Gray Goose," and walked away.

"Gray Goose?" Clarence whispered in confusion, "What did he mean by that?"

During this moment in time, Clovis had morphed into a new state of mind. Until now he played the role of the victim. In his mind, he thought that it was truly time for all adversaries to *pay the check*. What was his plan? Only Clovis knew the answer. All year long, Clovis wanted revenge. In the past, Clovis had to always take a backseat to his seemingly intelligent brother, Clarence. Intelligence in this household was always rewarded. Too bad Clovis was gifted with ample brawn. As far back as he could remember, Clovis never received a compliment for his honest efforts.

The Jump Rock

June 10, 1933

Clovis spent most of his time in his bedroom just laying on his bed and staring at the ceiling. As he laid there, he would whisper to himself ungodly thoughts – thoughts of revenge.

"Ohhh, they think that they are so smart. I'll show them who is smart. Wait until they get a load of me. Ohhh, slow down Clovis... you've got to have perfect timing. Oh yeah, you can pull this off," Clovis quietly spoke to himself as he waited for the perfect time.

School was out and Clarence and Clovis were down at the old mill pond. The day was hot, so now they were cooling off at the pond. While Clovis was wading, he looked up and saw Clarence had started his walk out to the ledge before making his jump down to the jump rock. Too bad for Clarence, Clovis had greased the jump rock one hour before his leap. Clovis could not resist the temptation of the moment. He quietly broke into Willard's favorite song.

"Beautiful dreamer, wake unto me, starlight and dewdrops are awaiting thee," he sang. After his song, Clovis began his own verbal assault to himself.

"Ohhhh, that's it, walk out there like a great big dummy. You'd better watch that first step – it's a killer! Ohhh, that's it, show ol' chicken foot how it's done.

You know, Clarence, this is all for your own good," he quoted Willard.

Finally, Clarence made the jump off the ledge and onto the greased jump rock. As expected, Clarence slipped and lost his footing. The fall was about twenty-five feet. His head smashed on the rocks below. He had fallen short of the mill pond. Clarence was dead.

Minutes later, Clovis left the wading pond. Soon there was someone coming down the path where Clarence had walked to the ledge. This was the same ledge where Clarence had fallen to his death. A familiar voice soon filled the silence of the mill pond.

"Ohhh, go tell Aunt Rhody, go tell Aunt Rhody, go tell Aunt Rhody that the old gray goose is dead."

"Ohhh, yeah, time to pay the check, brother," Clovis said.

Clovis walked down to the place where Clarence's body was laying. He quickly looked around to see if he was alone. He was. That was when he proceeded to follow through with his long-term plan. In his head, he believed the timing was perfect. So now, he had to act – and quickly.

Doppelganger: The Sheep Becomes the Wolf

Earlier in the afternoon, Lusinda looked out of her kitchen window and saw her two boys walk towards the old mill pond. Thirty minutes later, she saw one running back towards the house. She could tell by the color of his shirt that it was Clarence.

"There's been an accident! There's been an accident! Clovis slipped off the jump rock. He fell short of the pond and hit his head on a rock. He's not breathing," Clarence wheezed, short of breath.

Lusinda quickly called the hospital for an ambulance. Soon it arrived with the sheriff's car. The sheriff stopped at the house and made an assessment of the situation.

Meanwhile, the ambulance had taken a side road down to the accident at the mill pond. After the sheriff finished with a few questions for Lusinda, he ran out the back kitchen door and headed for the pond. Driving back to the side road was too time consuming.

Within four minutes, the sheriff had ran to the pond, only to see the paramedic slam the back door of the ambulance. The driver got in and drove off to the hospital.

At the accident scene, the sheriff walked around the base of the rock pile. Then, he walked around the side of the round rock ledge, which was overlooking the mill pond. From there, he noticed that the jump rock was covered with water. This water helped him conclude that an accident had indeed occurred.

An accident. Oh, if he only knew...

Back at the house, Lusinda was in the living room. The window was open. The sheriff came through the back door at the kitchen.

"Mrs. Hamley, Mrs. Hamley," Sheriff Beal called out.

"I'm out in the living room sheriff, please come in," Lusinda said.

Soon, Sheriff Beal and Lusinda were talking together in the living room. Little did they know that outside, next to the window was a pair of listening ears. Of course, it was Clovis. Yes, he had not finalized his new identity transfer, despite changing shirts with his twin brother.

"Mrs. Hamley, let me get this straight for my report. It was your son Clovis that slipped off of the jump rock onto the rocks below," Sheriff Beal said.

"Yes, yes, it was my son Clovis," Lusinda said. The sheriff stayed for about another ten minutes with Lusinda and then headed for the hospital. Once the sheriff was gone, in from the back door came "Clarence". Lusinda ran over to her son and embraced him.

"Oh, thank God you're safe, Clarence!" she said with relief. "I'm so glad it wasn't you."

His eyes seemed to pop right out of their sockets. Time seemed to stop dead in its tracks from the words spoken by his mother. And yet, her words only confirmed what he already knew. Clarence was her pride and joy. Nobody else.

The more things change, the more they stay the same.

About three months had passed by. Summer was gone. School was in progress. Lusinda noticed some unexpected changes in her son. Lusinda stopped Willard in the bedroom one night and asked him if he had a few minutes tomorrow to talk about some of the changes she had witnessed.

"Willard, let's meet in the living room tomorrow. We need to talk!" she said.

"Okay, let's make it about two o'clock," Willard said.

The next day came quickly and there they were in the living room.

"Willard, Clarence does not keep his room clean these days. His grades in school are marginal. He is getting a lot of C's. And did you notice last night at the table, he was talking with food in his mouth? He slouches in his chair. Something is just not right. That boy needs to snap out of it and make an extra effort," Lusinda said to Willard, visibly upset.

"Now, now, Lusinda, calm yourself down. The boy is only adjusting to the loss of his brother. Things will get back to normal. Give him some time. It will all work out. You've got to look at it this way – I no longer have to put my belt to Clovis's back anymore. That problem is gone. Everything is now going to be a lot easier. That boy was just plain stupid stubborn," Willard said with assurance.

"Why couldn't he have been more like Clarence?" Lusinda said.

"There you go, now that's the spirit. Everything will all work out for the best. Just give it some time," Willard said.

"You know, Willard, maybe I need to encourage Clarence. Maybe I need to get him to expand his horizons and see what success is within his reach. Yes, that's it," she said with a pause. "That should be fairly easy to do. After all, Clarence is not as stubborn as his brother was," Lusinda said.

Willard lingered on that trait. "Stubbornness, yes, that's what I need to put into one of my sermons on Sunday. After all, the good book clearly states, 'A stubborn man will always have wounds that need mending.' What a great sermon that will be," Willard said.

"You know Willard, I did my part. I tried to change that stubborn kid, but nothing worked. He seemed to be nothing but trouble. Trouble! That was his middle name. I tried to give him work, work, work, just to keep him busy, so he didn't have time to get into all that trouble," she asserted.

"Trouble! You don't have to explain that word to me. Clovis made me put my belt into overtime. His spankings were always for his own good. My own father preached that if you spare the rod, you will spoil the child," he said to his wife.

The living room window was once again open. Just beneath the window were fresh prints from the shoes of Clovis, once again.

Within minutes, the back screen door slammed. In came their son. He dropped his dirty shoes into the shoe box and walked straight into his messy bedroom and slammed the door.

Once again, he stopped to investigate the mirror at the door. With a low voice, he began to whisper to himself.

"Ohhhh, so I need to broaden my horizons? Ohhhh, I can make that happen."

All summer, "Clarence" spent countless hours pondering his glorious future – a self-made future, so he thought. He had lots to anticipate from the new vantage point of Clarence. Soon it was late September of 1933. The mood emanating throughout the country was that the happy days were here again. Clarence wanted to jump onto that bandwagon.

One Saturday afternoon, Willard came home with a friend named Alvin Wright. Alvin had a daughter that was the same age as Clarence. Her name was Sarah. Her and Clarence soon became very close friends. Sweethearts, in fact.

Alvin and Willard both were encouraging a permanent relationship between the two. Soon there was talk of marriage. Everybody seemed to be on board with this ideal scenario. Just ten months later, Clarence and Sarah were to be married in Willard's church.

Old Mill Pond Revisited

One summer day, there was the sound of someone coming down the pathway towards the ledge leading to the jump rock. This person was singing an old familiar tune.

"Go tell Aunt Rhody, go tell Aunt Rhody, go tell Aunt Rhody, the old gray goose is dead," Clarence sang. Clarence moved over towards the ledge and looked down at the jump rock.

"Ohhhh, life is oh-so-sweet!" Clarence just gave the jump rock a slight grin, then turned and walked away. That same afternoon, out at the cemetery where his brother was buried, Clarence approached the headstone of Clovis to speak a few choice words.

"Hi Clovis, or should I say Clarence? You remember me. You used to call me old chicken foot. Just to let you know, old chicken foot is going to get married soon. She's a real nice, sweet girl. You remember Sarah Wright? Wasn't she the girl you used to be sweet on? I gotta say, I'm glad that you can't make it to our wedding. Oh, I shouldn't say such bad things, but it sure is nice to hear. Oh well, I just stopped by to let you know that it sure is nice wearing all of those bright colored shirts of yours… Or should I say, *mine*! Guess what, I no longer have to hear mother say, 'Why can't you be like Clarence?' because, now *I am Clarence!* Oh, life is sweet. Goodbye gray goose! Sorry I greased the jump rock. What? You've got nothing to say!? I thought so. Oh, and one more thing, say hi to Jake," Clarence said with a smile.

Soon it was October 1, 1934. Lusinda came into the house about four o'clock. She was coughing and one of her hands was pressed on her chest during a strained coughing spell. Clarence came out of his room and witnessed the whole ordeal.

"I think I need to get some of my medicine from the end table by the couch. I have a great pain in my chest from all of this coughing," Lusinda said to Clarence. As she rushed towards the end table, she tripped on the rug. Suddenly, she was laying on the floor and stretching out her arm for the medicine bottle. The bottle was just out of her reach.

"Clarence, my meds, please get me my meds," she said. Clarence just stood there and thought for a moment. As he was thinking, he realized that they were alone in the house.

"Clarence, my meds, I need them," Lusinda pleaded.

"Oh now, you can reach them. I know you can. I just know you can. Why don't you just broaden your horizons and reach for success," Clarence taunted her.

Soon, Lusinda did just that. She was about to grab the bottle of meds when Clarence tapped it with his foot, making it once again, out of her reach.

"Ohhh, go tell Aunt Rhody, go tell Aunt Rhody, go tell Aunt Rhody that the old gray goose is dead," Clarence sang.

Lusinda looked up at Clarence. Her eyes were in shock. With her last words she said, "You're not Clarence! You're Clovis! You're Clovis!"

With both hands clutching her chest, she expired. Clarence stepped back from Lusinda's lifeless body. As he stood by the kitchen door, he stopped for a moment of silence, and he stared at her. This quiet time was not one of remorse, but a time to think and act quickly. He thought that it was not his place to discover her body, so he left the scene, hoping that somebody else would discover her body. Hopefully, it would be Willard.

And so it was. Within the hour, Willard came in through the kitchen door and discovered his perished wife. From that point on, it would be Willard's problem. The hospital, the coroner, the funeral, the cemetery, the new will and finally, Willard's death. But how was that going to take place? Only Clarence knew.

Fire and Brimstone Sermon

Three Sundays after Lusinda's funeral, Willard gave a sermon that revealed just what kind of a preacher man he was. Willard began his sermon rant like a drill sergeant.

"Everybody in this room is going to have his walk in the lake of fire! That's right! It's you, and you, and you." Willard pointed to a man and called him Jasper.

"That's right. And that includes you, you, and you." He pointed to a woman and called her Jezebel.

"The more you people sin with selfishness, the hotter the waters will be. So, what do you say, Jasper? What do you say, Jezebel? Need I remind you of Proverbs 29:1. 'He who hardens his heart and is often reproved shall suddenly be cut off without remedy.' You could die suddenly without any warning!"

The congregation seemed to absorb the dogma, but did Pastor Willard?

Clarence sat there in the pew and pondered everything that he had heard.

"That's it! That's it!" he whispered to himself with smug pleasure with his own cleverness. *That's how he's gotta go*, he thought.

What a sick and twisted creature Clovis had become. It was bad enough pretending that he was Clarence, but now, he was escalating out of control.

Death of Willard

October 31, 1934

"Say Clarence, what's shaking? I heard about all your bad luck. It was too bad about Clovis. He was a great guy. I always considered him to be a friend," Danny Sleeka said.

Danny was working at the county junk yard. His dad ran a used car junk yard on the outskirts of Wicker's Wood. Danny and his dad were both somewhat unsavory characters.

"So, what can I do you for, Clarence?" Danny's grammar was somewhat substandard.

"I need an old beater that can move when I punch the gas pedal, if you know what I mean," Clarence said.

"Let's talk money. How much do you want to spend?" Danny asked.

"No more than a hundred," said Clarence.

"Let's take a walk," Danny replied. They left Danny's trailer and stopped in front of an old beat-up Chevy.

"She looks like she has seen her best days," Clarence remarked.

"That's true, but a few days ago I took her out for a test drive. There's still some zip left," Danny said.

"Say, what's with all the holes in the back trunk lid?" Clarence asked.

"You are not going to let a few bullet holes bother you, are you? Danny asked.

"No not at all. What do you want for her?" Clarence asked.

"Earlier you said you were willing to part with a hundred. That's about what this gem is worth," Danny said with half a grin on his face.

"I think we both are on the same page. One hundred it is. I'll take it."

Clarence confirmed the deal with a handshake. He quickly handed Danny the hundred dollars.

"Oh, just so you know, there isn't any paperwork for this car. You are good to go," Danny said.

"Ohhh, life is sweet. Just what I needed!" Clarence whispered to himself as he went back to pick up his Chevy.

Once Clarence got into his new ride, he sped past Danny's trailer. Danny paused on his steps and witnessed Clarence's face as he exited the junk yard. He was talking to himself. Yes, Clarence was having a venting moment.

"Ohhhhhh, this is perfect. Absolutely perfect," Clarence said as he reached into his back pocket and pulled out that pair of lost gloves that his father had bought him a few years ago. The gloves were tight going on, but he felt compelled to wear them anyhow. Soon, he started to grip the steering wheel while his fingers continued to go up and down, as if he was playing the piano.

"Ohhhh, time to pay the check, old man. Time to pay the check," Clarence yelled out as he drove all the way back to the family farm.

There he was sitting in his Chevy about three hundred feet from the Hamley mailbox. He had been sitting there for about ten minutes when all of the sudden, out from the house came Willard. He was going out to pick up his daily mail from the box on the edge of the driveway. Willard was a creature of habit. He picked up his mail every day at the same time, at about two o'clock. Today, Willard had a lot of mail to pick up. He pulled out a large stack of mail and started to go through the stack while standing at the box.

Suddenly, without warning, there was a car driving at a high speed. The driver was heading straight down the gravel road towards the mailbox, or was it towards Willard? The person driving the car was wearing a pair of gloves. These gloves seemed to have a life of their own. The gloves started to play the piano on the steering wheel. The driver had a face of madness and anger. His eyes were popping out of their sockets. Sweat was pooling at his brow.

With a sick, vengeful burst of words, he said, "Ohhh, time to pay the check! Time to pay the check," Clarence chanted over and over.

As anticipated, Clarence's Chevy hit Willard. The car made a big thud. Willard went sailing into the ditch. He was dead. The car continued on its way for about a thousand feet and then, the road dipped down a sloped hill and disappeared. Soon he turned left onto a path that led to the old mill pond.

Once Clarence was on this path to the old mill pond, his demeanor seemed to calm down. He softly began to sing that old familiar tune.

"Go tell Aunt Rhody, go tell Aunt Rhody, go tell Aunt Rhody, the old gray goose is dead."

With a mocking tone to his voice, he expressed some old issues.

"Ohhhh, I suppose you know this was all for your own good. Ohhh, you made me do this. Ohhh, why can't you be more like Clarence? Ohhh, you've got nothing to say? I thought so. Say hi to Lusinda and Clarence," Clovis said as he parked the Chevy in some brush behind and old wooden shed at the pond.

Why did he park the car at the old mill pond? The pond was on Hamley property. Nobody really went there anymore. It was perfect, Clovis thought.

Meanwhile, Sarah and Betty, her best friend, came back to the farmhouse and saw Willard's dead body in the ditch along with some scattered mail. Betty called the sheriff. He arrived about thirty minutes later. Sheriff Beal stopped at the ditch by the mailbox and checked on Willard. Willard was a mangled mess. Sheriff Beal went into the house where Sarah and Betty were by the phone in the kitchen.

"Is there anybody here that can explain what happened?" Sheriff Beal asked the two ladies.

"When we drove up, I noticed some gravel dust in the air by the mailbox," Sarah said.

"I see. Well, maybe he was hit by a car. That does happen, you know. In fact, a few years ago a farmer was hit and killed at his mailbox over in the town of Prosper. It was listed as an accident," Sheriff Beal said.

"Sheriff Beal, let's go out into the living room. Have a seat on the couch." Betty said. Sarah was too shaken for conversation.

"Now Sarah, is there any bad blood in this family? Did Willard have any enemies?" the Sheriff asked.

"No, none that I am aware of," she answered.

"When was the last time that you talked to your husband? Did he give you any indication of a personal problem?" Sheriff Beal asked.

"No, to my knowledge, everything was normal," Sarah said. Suddenly, Sarah started to cry. Betty came over to console her. Sheriff Beal also made an effort.

Just outside the living room window, a window that was open a few inches, Clovis was listening.

"Ohhh, show time. It is time for me to make my entrance. Ohhh, the sheriff is fishing for some bad blood. Ohhh, not me. Not even!" Clovis whispered to himself as he came in from the back kitchen door.

The Smell of Onions

As Clovis's alter-ego stepped into the living room, his eyes were all watered up with tears. He was playing the part of a grieving son. His performance was excellent. Soon the sheriff was out of questions. He left the farmhouse after the ambulance departed with Willard's body.

When things calmed down, Sarah went out into the kitchen. Over by the door, she smelled onions. What she didn't know was that Clarence had cut open an onion and squeezed some onion juice into his eyes to make tears. Yes, all those tears were fake.

At this point in time, Clovis had thought that he had pulled off a masterful impersonation of Clarence. Could anybody stop him now? He didn't think so.

Willard's Funeral

November 3rd, 1934

The church that Willard long preached to his congregation became the place for his funeral. There were many church members present to grieve his loss, at the Sacred Heart Church in the village of Prosper Missouri.

After the church service, there was to be a viewing in the Fellowship Hall next door. The funeral director approached Clarence and asked him one question.

"During this kind of service, we typically have music. Is there any favorite song that Pastor Willard had?"

Clarence paused and spoke up.

"Beautiful Dreamer."

"Yes, that would be his favorite tune. I am sure of it." Clarence said to the funeral director, thinking back on the beatings he endured to this melody at the choice and hands of his father.

The past few years had taken quite a toll on the Hamley family, which Sarah married into not expecting such chaos. Death never seemed to take a holiday.

Sarah's marriage to Clarence did not last very long. Only four months (July 6th to November 5th, 1934).

One day, Sarah had a mysterious exchange with Betty while on the back porch.

"Betty, do you remember our conversation at Willard's funeral?" Sarah asked.

"Yes, I do!" Betty responded.

"Remember when I asked you if you noticed any differences between Clarence and Clovis?" Sarah asked.

"Clovis used to wear an old ring that he found at the beach when he visited his Uncle Roy in South Carolina. Clarence always hated to wear jewelry, but yesterday I noticed that he was wearing the same ring," Sarah said.

"Oh Sarah, it is probably nothing." Betty assured her.

"Betty, lately I have been having very bad headaches. I feel like my life is draining from my body. I always want to lay down. In fact, I feel one coming on right now. I think I need to lay down. Please help me to my bed," Sarah pleaded.

A few days later Betty came over to check on Sarah. They both sat on the back porch swing. As time went by, once again, Sarah felt a very bad headache coming on.

"Betty, could you help me to my bed?" Sarah asked. Once again, Betty did so.

"Come over closer to my bed, so I won't have to speak so loud," Sarah asked. Betty moved closer to Sarah.

"Betty, you have been my closest friend since childhood. We both go way back to Wickers Wood together. I consider you as part of my family. There are a few things I need to tell you," She whispered.

"What's that?" Betty asked.

"Betty, if anything ever happens to me, I want you to take care of Clarence. He has such bad luck in life. Promise me! Promise me!" Sarah desperately begged of her friend.

"Sarah, please don't talk like that. Everything is going to turn out okay. You'll see." Betty said.

"Lately, Clarence has been acting sort of strange," Sarah said softly.

"How strange?" Betty asked.

"Yesterday, when I was laying in bed, I heard him softly singing," Sarah explained.

"Singing what?" Betty asked.

"*Go Tell Aunt Rhody*," Sarah said.

"Now, that's a strange song to be singing," Betty said with a surprised look.

"Betty, there is something else. Lately, I have been finding a few hidden bottles of brandy. Clarence never drank when I first met him," she said.

"Oh Sarah, if I had all of the bad luck that Clarence has had to put up with, I'd drink too. You might be overreacting. I'm sure of it," Betty said with assurance.

Without warning, Sarah's strength diminished. With one last surge, she sat up and looked straight into Betty's eyes and softly said, "Please take care of my dear Clarence." She then fell back into the bed and died. Betty was completely caught off guard.

"This can't be happening. What? Sarah, Sarah, Sarah, please say something!" Betty pleaded.

Nothing but silence overtook the room. Betty ran for the phone, but it was too late. There was nothing to do but call the hospital. The ambulance came out and took away Sarah, Betty's dear, sweet friend.

By this time, Betty cried for three days straight. She was confounded. How could someone who loved unconditionally fail to have a full, rich life? Betty and Sarah shared the very same beliefs, and in a sense, she felt a piece of herself symbolically die too. Sarah was only guilty of wanting to love and be loved in return.

35

For many weeks, Betty remembered the sound of Sarah's voice and her last words, *Betty, please take care of my dear Clarence.*

In her mind, that is what she had to do. Eventually, about 8 months later, that is what developed. Betty married Clarence. Was it love or was it a dying friend's request she had to fulfill? Only Betty knew that answer. They were wed on the 7th of July 1935.

Betty Begins New Life with Clarence

July 7th, 1935

Once Betty became the wife of Clarence, the following two years seemed to become unbearable. All of the good things that Clarence thought would happen once he became the sole heir of the Hamley property never materialized. The Dust Bowl made his property worthless. The general store and hardware store wanted their accounts to be paid. But Clarence had no cash available. Somehow, he always had money for whiskey. So, whiskey it was, and plenty of it. Clarence had many reasons to drink. The dead bodies had piled up, but remorse? There was none! In fact, he blamed most of his shortcomings on poor Betty. She had become worn out, from just two years of drunken Clarence.

She often sat on the porch swing and asked herself a very pointed question.

Betty, why are you staying?

The only answer was always on the edge of her tongue. It was Sarah's request. Since Betty was taught from childhood that longsuffering was reality, she had in her mind, no choice. She stayed.

The only good thing about the Hamley farm was the fact that it had running water down at the old mill pond. The land that was next to the pond area was still tillable. So, Betty had a large area of land cut out for a garden. That garden produced enough food to can for the many months ahead. They lived off of this garden, right though the Dust Bowl years.

Leona's Visit

Amidst the despair of the Dust Bowl years, life on the Hamley Farm was still hard. Jobs were scarce and land prices were at the bottom for most farmers. But, somehow, the Hamley farm held on — only because there was running water down at the mill pond. Most farms did not have such a gift. The Hamley farm was a little more valuable because of it. However, making money was of no concern to Clarence. He was busy living in the bottom of his whiskey bottle.

As the years passed by, from 1935 to 1938, hard times seemed to be everywhere. Tension between Betty and Clarence seemed to be excessive. It was hard not to notice this adversarial relationship. Things seem to boil over one summer day in 1938.

"Betty, where is my bottle? I thought that I told you to keep it on the first pantry shelf. I don't see it there!" Clarence shouted.

"I've been busy, busy, busy, doing other things, like the laundry, the floors, the rugs, and now you've got me feeding the chickens. Where is this all going? It seems like you have got me running in circles. When will this all stop? You don't want a wife. You want a personal slave," Betty vented.

Clarence went over to the pantry to find his bottle of whiskey. It wasn't there. He went to his bedroom and found another half full bottle of whiskey under the mattress at the foot of his bed. He grabbed his bottle and went outside to the garage, slamming the door very hard as he left the house.

In the meantime, while Clarence was in the garage getting drunk, there was a knock at the front door. Betty went out through the living room and answered the knock. As soon as the door opened, Betty's surprise made her yell.

"Leona, well I'll be! What a great surprise!" Betty said to her cousin, Leona.

Before long, both of them were sitting at the kitchen table having coffee and cookies. When in came Clarence, he quickly stared at Betty and slurred out some crass words.

"What's she doing here?"

"This is my cousin, Leona. I haven't seen her in several years. We are just having coffee and cookies," Betty nervously replied.

"Well, see to it that's all that's happening. We can't take on any more problems," Clarence said, as he went back to the garage to drink the rest of his whiskey.

Betty and Leona just stood there speechless for a quiet moment.

"Betty, maybe I should come back at a better time?" Leona suggested, out of politeness.

"A better time? Let's make it Saturday at three o'clock. Clarence is usually passed out by then. We will talk then," Betty said.

Saturday came and it was as Betty predicted — Clarence was passed out drunk. Betty went out on the back porch and sat in the double swing.

"Betty, I don't want to pry, but is everything all right?" Leona asked.

"Is everything all right? I guess you could say that it is better than a sharp stick in the eye. Whenever Clarence drinks, nothing is ever right. And he drinks all the time. So, life is getting unbearable. I was hoping that things would get better now that we have a son. I guess I was hoping that we would be a normal family. My son Farris is the only joy that I have left. Every day I read to him a chapter in the Bible. He really looks forward to it," Betty said.

"Why does Clarence drink so much?" Leona asked.

"I don't exactly know. Sometimes he just sits in the living room and talks in a low voice. It is almost like he is talking to someone in the room," Betty said.

"What does he say?" Leona asked.

"Oh, he says things like, 'Sit up straight, don't talk with food in your mouth. Where are your gloves. Ohhhh, time to pay the check.' None of it makes any sense," Betty said.

"Betty, I feel your pain, but tomorrow I am leaving on the train for Los Angeles. I have a job there that I need to take. It is a schoolteacher position. That's what I trained for," Leona said.

The very next day, Leona was gone. Life went back to being unbearable for Betty. In her mind, she thought life was now at her worst. But that was soon to change…or was it?

Bobby Joe Hamley Visits

May 1939

Summer days can be hot and unforgiving when you live in a dust bowl on the edge of hell. Clarence would try to cool the edge with a seat in a swing on the front porch and a bottle of *Southern Comfort*. Oh patiently, he waited for the next cool breeze. A breeze that drove up in a brand-new Cadillac. It was his cousin, Bobby Joe Hamley. He drove up like he was on a mission, then suddenly stopped. Quietly, he opened the driver door, and a cowboy boot exited the car.

"Well, howdy, Cousin Clarence. How's it rolling? Are you hanging in there? It's been a spell since we last met. I see that the dust bowl hasn't wiped you out," Bobby Joe said.

"Yeah, we've managed to keep our stomachs full," Clarence replied.

"I can believe that. You always did enjoy a good full glass of whisky," Bobby Joe said with a laugh.

"What brings you back to the old neighborhood, Bobby Joe. I thought that you hung your shingle down in Texas," Clarence said with a smirk.

"That be true for sure. I am here just for a short trip, Clarence," Bobby Joe said.

"Say Bobby, how did you come by such a great looking car? That must have set you back quite a bit," Clarence said.

"Clarence, that is not just a car. Come on over here and see for yourself. Here, I'll roll down the window. You just stick your head inside and take a deep breath. You smell that?" Bobby asked.

"Yeah, smells brand new."

"No, Clarence. What you smell is money. That's the strong smell of money, and lots of it. You could have some of that too. You do like money, don't you, Clarence?" Bobby Joe asked.

"Yeah, these last few years have been draining the old bank account. The bills are overdue, and Betty is now caring for our child," Clarence rattled on.

"I think I could help you out," Bobby Joe said.

"Let's go in the house, come on Bobby Joe, let's talk," Clarence asked, quite curious as to the details of the money business.

"Say Bet, bring me my new bottle of *Southern Comfort*. Bobby needs to wet his whistle. Then you can go out into the back yard. Me and Bobby need to talk a spell in private," Clarence said.

Betty came up to the table and slammed the bottle down and left the kitchen to go outside.

"What's with her? Is she angry or something?" Bobby Joe asked.

"Oh, she is just being her bitchy self," Clarence slurred out.

"What I said earlier is sure and true. I do enjoy helping out kin folk with money problems," Bobby Joe said.

"How could you help me, Bobby?" Clarence asked.

"I heard that you have had a string of bad luck with your folks dying. Willard must have left you with about a thousand acres of good land. Good land is hard to come by these days. You could sell some of that land and make your money work for you the same way it worked for me, Clarence," Bobby Joe said.

"Okay, how so? How did you make your money work for you, Bobby Joe?"

"Come a little bit closer. Not many people know this, but I invested in an oil rig in Texas. It paid off. That could happen to you. You just got to be ready when it's time. The time is now, Clarence. Our company is currently investing in a new drill spot in Midland. If you got, let's say, about $20,000, you could double that in about two months time," Bobby Joe said while confidently sitting back in his chair.

It didn't take much talk to convince Clarence. This whole deal was too good to be true. In short order, Clarence sold half of his land to a rich farmer who had been trying to get his land for some time. Everything seemed to fall into place. He got a good price, then wrote out a personal check to Bobby Joe, who drove back to Texas and disappeared into thin air.

Three months later, Bobby Joe's father in Missouri near the Hamley farm had suffered a tractor accident. Bobby Joe came back from Texas to check on him. While visiting in Wickers Wood, Bobby Joe's car was found on the road to Spiney's Ridge.

Where was Bobby Joe? Nobody had that answer. One day Clarence came home to his farmhouse and stopped by the woodshed. From there he opened the trunk lid and tossed a dirty shovel towards the shed, slammed the trunk, went into the house and made himself a hobo sandwich – washing it down with a long swig of whiskey.

As he was sitting there in the kitchen chair, Betty came in and asked him where he had been. "I've been out feeding some worms." Clarence replied.

A week later, Bobby Joe's dad had died in a nursing home. Relatives came from all over, but there was no Bobby Joe. Nobody knew where he was – except perhaps, Clarence. Bobby Joe had a reputation of being a free spirit. He traveled quite a bit. He could have been anywhere. Maybe the authorities needed to look in the wooded area up on Spiney's Ridge.

Joe Finney's Visit

September 1940

About a year later after the visit from Bobby Joe, there was a knock at the door.

"Say, Clarence, there is somebody here that says he's Joe Finney." Betty said.

"So, what are you waiting for, show him in!" Clarence yelled back.

"Finney!" Clarence exclaimed as he came around the corner with excitement. "How the hell are you?" he asked.

"Okay, I guess. Better than a sharp stick in the eye!" Finney replied.

"I know what you are saying…" Clarence said.

"I've been working for a tool supply company down in Atlanta, until I got fired for stealing tools," Finney said.

"Well, were you stealing?" Clarence asked.

"Of course!" Finney said.

"So, what's your next move?" Clarence asked.

"Oh, I was thinking about going up to Alaska and getting a job on a fishing boat. They tell me that those guys make a lot of money every day. Money! Lots of easy money." Finney said.

"There's nothin' *easy* about that kind of money," Clarence said skeptically.

"Yeah, but I'm still in great shape. I can take a few good days of hard work," Finney said with assurance.

"Say Betty, go into the pantry and get my new bottle of whiskey, and then find yourself out in the garden. Me and Finney need to talk for a spell – alone!" Clarence said.

Betty got Clarence's bottle and walked over to the kitchen table and slammed the bottle down and slammed the kitchen door as she left.

"What's with her? Is she angry or something?" Finney said.

"Oh, she is just being her bitchy self," Clarence said with a slur.

"How about you Clarence? How do you keep the wolf away from the front door?" Finney asked.

"You want to know how I pay for this mess, don't you?" Clarence said.

At this point the drinks were flowing. It didn't take much; they were both drinking on empty stomachs.

Finney waved his half full glass of whiskey and slurred out that same question one more time.

"How do you survive, Clarence?" Finney asked.

"Oh, when others make me zig! I zag. And I make them pay the check. Ohhhh yeah, I make them pay the check is what I do," Clarence said with a smug smile.

"Here, Finney, it looks like your glass needs a refill," he slurred.

After about thirty minutes of conversation, they both were fairly sauced with booze.

"Say Clarence, you didn't tell me how you make your money," Finney slurred.

"Land, land, land – that's what my father left me. He left me everybody else's land. He made himself the president of the church's housing board. Him and three other members swindled old ladies out of their family farms by having them turn over their land in fat wills. He only preyed upon the weak-minded who had no kin. Today, I lease out most of that farmland to sharecroppers," Clarence said.

"So how much land did Willard get?" Finney asked, somewhat surprised.

"Oh, about a thousand acres. Today I only have about half that left over," Clarence said.

"Five hundred acres left! What happened?" Finney questioned.

"Deeds, I told you, deeds. Say, you ask too many questions. Here, have some whiskey," Clarence said as he spilled whiskey as he reached to fill Finney's glass. "Oh, I made a mess."

"Betty, come back here and wipe up this mess!" Clarence yelled at the top of his voice through the window.

Betty came in from the garden and stood there and shook her head with disgust. Not saying a word. She was used to suffering in silence. That was her way. She went back to her garden.

"Say, Clarence, I'm really sorry to hear all that bad news about your family. First, there was Clovis, then Lusinda, then Willard, then Sarah…all gone. Did they ever find out who killed Willard?" Finney asked curiously.

"I don't like your tone of voice. You just never mind about that, you hear?" Clarence said as he took another drink.

"Oh, Clarence, I really miss that Clovis. He was a good old boy. We had a few good times together. His parents must have been proud of him. Why, I remember one time we were removing some nails from some boards over at the old Blake Farm. Willard wanted us to fix her woodshed. Clovis was removing a nail and he hit the thumb on his left hand. Later on, that thumbnail was split into two nails. It never did grow back into one thumbnail," Finney said.

Just then, Finney looked down at Clarence's left thumb. It was split into two nails. Clarence saw Finney stare at his thumb. He quickly covered it up so Finney wouldn't see it anymore.

"You know Finney. I once knew a man that kept sticking his nose into places where it didn't belong," Clarence said.

"What happened to him?" Finney asked.

"Well, one day they found him buried in a potato patch in the next county. It wasn't a very pleasant sight. Parts of his nose were missing and the worms had eaten half his body," Clarence said as he waved his glass full of whiskey.

Finney's eyes grew large. He got up and walked towards the kitchen door to make his exit. He stopped and made a few remarks before leaving.

"You know Clarence, I think I'll go over to visit Alice next door. By tomorrow, I think that I am going to be up in Alaska with that job on a fishing boat," Finney slurred out.

Joe Finney did just that. The next day Betty looked out of the kitchen window and saw Finney in the driveway, walking down Sailor's Hill. He got into his car and drove away. He was never seen again. There are some who say that he fell off a fishing boat in Alaska and drowned. Nobody knew for sure.

The New Preacher

May 1941

On April 2nd, 1935, the Sacred Heart Church of Prosper, Missouri was finally assigned a new pastor. His name was Pastor Michael Morris. His tenure at this church was to last until his retirement on April 4th, 1941.

For the next six years, Pastor Morris preached a standard and rigid doctrine from the scriptures. But that was all about to change.

On March 10th, 1941, Superintendent Vance Sheldon called Pastor Morris from his church office in Cape Girardeau, Missouri.

"Michael, this is Van. The reason that I am calling is to ask you for a recommendation on the vacancy at your church. Do you have any input? If you do, I would like to hear it. Your advice would be greatly appreciated. Who would you recommend?" Superintendent Sheldon inquired.

"There is one person that comes to mind. Pastor C.B. Lukka. I am sorry to say that I have never met him. But I do know him by reputation. He is a part-time, fill-in pastor. I am sure that he would accept this position. However, there would be one drawback," Michael said.

"And what's that?" Van asked.

"Well, Pastor Lukka does have an… unorthodox presentation of scripture. Sometimes he can get a little off script if you know what I mean. Would he be a good fit? I don't know. Only time would tell," Michael said.

"If that's the case, I need to see him address his congregation. Perhaps you could join me this Sunday? It might prove to be very interesting. We could both go early to the church and sit in the last row. That way we would not draw too much attention," Van suggested.

"I think that we can make that happen. I'll meet you out in the parking lot about ten minutes before the service," Michael said, as he hung up the phone.

Meanwhile, back at the church office, Molly the church secretary, asked Bo a personal question.

"Bo, did you always want to be a preacher?" she wondered out loud.

"Oh, no! My absolute dream job would be to be a farmer on the top of a hill, overlooking a valley. There is something so magical about sitting on the back porch and watching the sun go down after a hard day's work," Bo said.

"Do you even know of such a place?" Molly asked.

"Yes, my Uncle Alton's Farm..."

C.B. Lukka's First Sermon at Sacred Heart Church

May 1941

Finally, Sunday arrived. Pastor Bo Lukka called in the choir leader, Leigh Lang.

"Leigh, remember what we talked about yesterday? We need to do this. Are you still okay with that?" Bo asked.

"Yes! I will do what you asked," she replied.

"Okay, let's go over it again so that we're both on the same page. Once I start my sermon, I want you to start playing this record on the phonograph. It's called *Beautiful Dreamer*. Play it softly when I give my introduction. This song will put everybody at ease," he insisted.

"I'll do that," Leigh assured Bo.

Bo began his sermon right on time.

"Hello, I would like to introduce myself," Lukka started while the music began. "My name is Claremont Bob Lukka. For years, people used to call me C.B. Lukka or just plain C.B. for short. I would be more at ease though if you just called me Bo. I guess that everybody wants to see how a new 27-year-old preacher preaches. I hope that I am not a big disappointment."

"My sermons do have an element of surprise and candor. I do not want to offend anybody, but I will not shy away from what I think is right, even if it does ruffle some feathers. Most of all, I do want people to ask some basic questions about their faith. Questions like, 'Why do I do the things that I do?' or 'Why are we faced daily with sin and suffering and death?' Oh, if we could just sit down and have those questions answered..."

"Today's sermon is called *Pertempto Fidem*. For those of you that don't read Latin, and I believe that's everybody here...*pertempto* means 'to test' and *fidem* means 'faith.' Together they mean 'to test your faith,' and that, my friends, is the reason why we are all here on Earth. The Earth is not our playground. Earth is a place where souls are sent to be harvested. That includes you, me, and everybody that is made by our maker."

"I see some of you are shaking your heads. You probably are asking yourself why a loving God would make evil men and evil deeds." There was a quiet pause with music playing softly. Back in the church, Bo Lukka continued his sermon.

"How could such a horrible thing happen? I cannot answer that question without referring to the scriptures in the Bible. For those of you that have your Bible handy, look up 2 Corinthians 4:4. It clearly says that the God of this age blinds the minds of those who do not believe. That, my friends, is not the God of the age that is to come, for He is a holy God. Don't go blaming Him for sin, suffering and death," Pastor Lukka warned as the music began playing gradually louder.

"Here is something that you really don't expect to hear. This congregation does not need Pastor Bo Lukka for your salvation. I cannot make anybody a true believer. Only you and the direction of the Holy Spirit can do that. And yes, it's nice that we have a full house today, with all thirty-two church members are present. That's great! However, perfect attendance is not a requirement for salvation."

"You may be wondering 'So, what can I do?' and 'How can I be saved?' My advice to you would be to find a private place and with a pure heart, ask the Holy Spirit to come in and be the director of your life. Ask him to make you born again in the Spirit. Bo Lukka can't do that for you. You have to knock on the Lord's door, and He will invite you in." C.B. Lukka said.

Van looked over at Michael and said, "Outside – we need to talk."

Pastor Michael Morris and Van Sheldon stood up in the last row and left the sanctuary. Outside they began to talk.

"You know, Michael, Bo Lukka might not be such a great fit in this church. How many pastors tell their congregation that they don't need him? I think it would be surprising if anybody showed up next week for the services," Van said.

"You might have a point there. What do you want to do?" Pastor Michael said.

"Let's give him a couple of weeks and see what happens. I want to see how this plays out," Van said.

Both Pastors Michael Morris and Van Sheldon left the church grounds. Back in the church, the service continued.

Sitting in the third row from the center front was Betty and Clarence. Betty had insisted that both of them attend church to hear the new pastor. Clarence clearly did not want to come, but at the last minute he changed his mind and went along with Betty.

"...and there is one more thing that I need to talk about, and that is 'hardened hearts.' The Good Book says in Proverbs 29:1, 'He who hardens his heart is often reproved, shall be suddenly cut off without remedy. That means you could be killed without warning," Lukka said as the music played louder.

Up until that point, Clarence was not paying much attention to the sermon. Suddenly, his ears perked up and he started to look at the exit door.

Betty turned her face towards Clarence, and she nudged him to turn back around. Clarence complied. Pastor Bo Lukka started to draw the service down, but he left the congregation with some encouraging words:

"My fellow friends in Christ, when you leave here today, I want you to find a quiet place and then ask the Holy Spirit to come in and be director of your life. And always remember the scripture 1 John 4:4. 'Greater is He that is in me, than he that is in the world.' Amen."

Outside at the end of the service, Betty turned towards Clarence and asked what he thought of the new pastor.

"Did you think that his sermon was relevant to our lives?"

"What does he know about sin, suffering, and death? I bet you that he has had nothing but a charmed life. He probably was his mom and dad's favorite son. And that song he played in the service... you can't make every problem just go away with a happy song. That song, oh, how I hate that song," Clarence said.

"Why do you hate that song?" Betty asked, confused.

"It reminds me of a pair of gloves," Clarence said angrily.

"A pair of gloves! That doesn't make any sense. Perhaps we should go next week? You might have a better experience then," Betty said.

"You can go if you like. Not me! No thanks! Next week he probably is going to tell me that everything is for my own good. Let's go. I've had enough," Clarence said as he rushed towards his car.

While in the car, when Clarence was driving back to the Hamley Farm, Betty started up a conversation about what she overheard on the steps of the church as she was leaving.

"Clarence, did you hear Pastor Bo's answer to a question that was asked outside the church?"

"No! What was it?" Clarence asked.

"A man asked, 'I swear, drink, smoke and raise hell. Is there any hope for me?' and Pastor Bo just paused a moment and said, 'Sir, the Good Book says that whatever overcomes you in the world, to that you will become a slave. In the Lord's gospel, he also says that He has overcome the world. I am the way, the truth, and the life.'"

"Aw, that's all just pulpit poetry. When was he ever tested?" Clarence questioned to Betty in the car.

As they continued on their way home, Betty whispered to herself, "*I have overcome the world.*" Clarence heard her.

"Just forget about all that stuff. I believe in things that I can hold with my own hands," he said in anger. Once they got home, silence filled the room.

Back at the Church

"The Meeting"

Outside on the church lawn two members, Asa Archer and Buford Timmers, stood.

"Who does he think he is? What kind of preacher says that the congregation doesn't need him? Maybe down the road he is going to say that he doesn't need our finance committee because he can do it all himself," Buford said.

"Now, Buford, you are getting yourself all worked up over nothing. Next week he just might mellow out. Let's wait and see," Asa said with an open mind.

"Okay, but I gotta tell ya, I don't like it," Buford said as he walked away.

C.B. Lukka's Second Sermon

May 7, 1941

Soon the following Sunday came and there they were. It was Betty and Clarence sitting about four rows back near the center of the church.

"I can't believe that you talked me into coming again. Coming here to listen to C.B. Lukka is a waste of time. What's in it for me? How's he gonna help me?" Clarence asked Betty.

"Clarence, you have changed over the years. When I first met you, you were so kind and thoughtful. What happened?" Betty asked.

"What happened? Life! Too much of a hard life. I just bet you that Bo Lukka wouldn't know anything about that. Who is going to trust a guy like that?" Clarence quietly ranted.

Betty just turned and faced the alter. She didn't want to spoil the outing. Soon the sanctuary was filled to capacity. There was standing room only. The attendance went from last week's thirty-two to now fifty-two worshipers.

C.B. Lukka came out and stood at the pulpit and paused with a surprised look.

"Wow! Hello my friends, hello. I never thought that telling you that you didn't need me would be so attractive to you," Lukka said to the full-house that laughed in reply.

"You know, last week, I couldn't help but notice that there were two men in the back row that got up and left after I said that. That's okay, I guess my words didn't pass the spinach test. I suppose some of you are wondering what I mean by 'Spinach Test,' so here it is..."

"Suppose I found out that you hated spinach and that I tied you to a chair and then started to force feed you spinach. As I was force feeding you spinach, I told you that this was all for your own good. Suppose you broke away and freed yourself. Would you then, go out and buy more spinach? I don't think so. And such isn't the way of the Lord. He is not going to force you to the cross. Why? That's your hour of decision. He stands at the door waiting for your knock. He wants you to come by your own free will. It doesn't matter who you are or where you are – it is your choice."

"You know the trouble with all of us is quite simple. We all want our own way. Everybody sees their own truth. That is why we are smothered with sectarianism. We instead need to focus on all the good things that we have in common. We need to call out sin for what it really is – rebellion against God. And who is the author of all this sin? It is Satan. The Good Book says that he is the author of all confusion. That is, confusion between man and man, and between God and man."

"And so my friends, you ask yourself, what does C.B. Lukka want me to do? What's my advice? I can only say, *pray, believe, do.* Your choice? Well, that's your hour of decision. Amen."

Because of the large crowd, Bo Lukka made the sermon extra short, but added, "I see one of last week's walkouts has returned. That's great. Perhaps there is some hope in my sermons," Bo Lukka said.

Now at the end of the service, the music was playing quite loud. *Beautiful Dreamer* brought back painful memories for Clarence. He was now extremely stressed.

Before everybody left the sanctuary, Bo Lukka made an announcement.

"Next week, our sermon will be about Numbers 32:23 in the Old Testament. I intend on having a discussion on some of the unresolved discrepancies in this church. Hopefully this will give us some peace of mind," Bo said.

Once the church members came outside, Buford called Asa over to the oak tree for a few serious words.

"Asa, I don't like this. What does he mean with 'discrepancies?' And that scripture? You've got a Bible. Look it up now!" Buford demanded. Asa opened his Bible and went to the scripture. *Be sure to know your sins will find you out.*

"What does he mean? He will find us out! Out!? Find out about what?" Asa yelled.

"Keep your voice down," Buford said.

"I've got nothing to hide," Asa blurted out.

"Oh, you've got nothing to hide, do you? What about all that property that Pastor Willard divided up between us from all those property sales? You were the one that got the Widow Saunders to sign over all of her property to the church, but what she didn't know was that sales money was never recorded into the church coffers. Willard got a personal check and you got five hundred acres of the homestead land. That was all free money and a chunk of it went into your pocket. So, let's not get so high and mighty, Asa. You are in it up to your eyebrows," Buford said.

"I didn't get as much as Willard," Asa said defensively. "He got a thousand acres. What did you get?" Asa asked.

"None of your business, Asa," Buford said.

"So, what are we going to do?" Asa asked.

Buford put both of his hands on top of his head and brushed them down over his face.

"I don't know!" Buford said.

"This is all too much, too fast," Asa said.

"Okay, let's meet by the pond, up on Spiney's Ridge, tomorrow at noon," Buford suggested.

"I'll be there. I've got an hour for lunch," Asa said.

"An hour for lunch? You're the boss. Make it as long as you need. This is important!" Buford said as he departed.

The following afternoon Asa arrived before Buford. Suddenly, a car came up the road and stopped. Out stepped Buford, but Buford was not alone. He had brought along a passenger. This passenger was a good-sized, young man. He was about 6'3" tall and weighted about 250 pounds.

Asa had a few choice words for Buford in their approach.

"What's with the kid? I thought this was going to be a private meeting," Asa said.

"Relax, he has the same problem we have," Buford said.

"I still don't like it!" Asa said to Buford.

"You don't have to like it. Just don't become a problem, you hear?" Buford snapped back.

"Say kid, what's your name?" Asa asked.

"Don't call me kid. If you do, I'll rearrange your smile," he said.

"So, what's your name?" Asa asked.

"My friends call me C.W. You can just call me Caleb," he said.

"So, Caleb, are you from around here? I haven't seen you around," Asa said.

"I've lived here since 1934. We bought a farm ten miles south of here," Caleb said.

"So, I take it that your father is a farmer. What does he farm?" Asa asked.

"Right now, fertilizes worms. He's dead."

"What did he die of?" Asa asked.

"Oh, he drowned in the bottom of a whiskey bottle. Good riddance! He treated my mother like she was some kind of slave. He tossed her around like she was a rag doll. Why she took it all in silence, I don't know. But, one thing is sure, if I did something wrong, she always took the blame for me. She was a saint. I would do anything to protect her. Nobody, and I mean nobody, is going to come along and take away her home. Nobody!" Caleb said.

"I see, well I guess that's why we are all here. Everybody has a stake in the situation," Asa said.

"Okay, that's enough chit chat. Let's get down to business. Say Asa, will you stop shaking. You make coffee nervous. Stop it right now!" Buford said.

"I can't help it!" Asa said.

"You can't help it? I thought you were a doctor!" Buford said.

"I'm not a doctor, I'm a veterinarian," Asa replied.

"I...don't...care. Get a hold of yourself or I'll give you something to really worry about," Buford said in anger.

"I think that we are going to be okay. C.B. Lukka has got nothing in writing," Buford said.

"Oh, Buford, there is something I think that I should mention," Asa said.

"Oh, what now? What is it?" he asked.

"Ah, Molly down at the church office told me a couple of years ago that Willard kept a personal diary," Asa said.

"What? Why didn't you say that last week when we were talking outside of church?" Buford yelled at Asa.

"I didn't think it was important," Asa cried.

"Unbelievable! Do you think that embezzling money from church funds gives you a free pass out of jail? Do you think that showing a profit from a crime is going to keep your house, your land, your good name? It's all going up in smoke, mister. You...had...better... wake...up...and smell...the coffee. You have jail bird written all over your face," Buford said.

"So, what are we going to do about that?" Asa asked.

"Well, Asa, I want you to go back to the church office and revisit that conversation you had with Molly – about that diary. Find out where it is right now. Better yet, I'll do it myself. You're a nervous wreck," Buford said.

The very next day, Buford waited for Bo Lukka to leave the church. Buford knew that Bo had a funeral that afternoon. Once Bo left the church, Buford went into the church office to talk with Molly.

"So Molly, is Bo around?" Buford asked.

"Oh, he went out to the Hamley Farm to straighten out some issues. Bo is doing a funeral today at two o'clock. Pastor Michael Morris is going to be here to assist with the service," Molly said.

"So, Molly, I see that Bo Lukka's office has been changed around. Looks like you did a good job. Did you happen to find anything from the past?" Buford asked.

"Oh yeah, it is funny you should mention that. We did find a book when we moved that heavy oak desk away from the wall," Molly said.

"What kind of book was it?" Buford asked.

"It looked like a diary or something. You know, I bet it was Willard's diary. He kept a financial record of all the happenings," Molly said.

"So, Molly, do you know where that diary is now?" Buford asked.

"I saw it on Bo's desk this morning, but when he left the office this morning, he said that he was going out to the Hamley Farm. He must have taken the diary with him. When he left, he said that he had to clear something up," Molly said.

"I see," Buford said as he left in a hurry.

Without delay, Buford got into his dark black Chevy and headed for the Hamley Farm. Buford was not alone on Woodland Drive Road. Coming from the other direction was a monster from Wickers Wood.

As this monster was driving, he was whispering to himself, "It's time to pay the check, it's time to pay the check."

Suddenly, there was Bo Lukka. He had a car behind him and a car coming at him from the other direction.

Bo Lukka made a left turn onto County Road 15 and headed towards the direction of Spiney's Ridge. And that was the last time that the people of Prosper ever saw him again.

The Pond up at Spiney's Ridge

Two weeks after the disappearance of Bo Lukka, here was Clarence sitting at a fishing hole up on Spiney's Ridge.

For a brief moment, Clarence reached down in his bait bucket and grabbed a worm to put on his hook.

"Oh, you really are a big and fat worm. I fed you real good, didn't I?" Clarence whispered to himself.

Suddenly Clarence realized that he wasn't alone. Along came another fisherman. He sat down about twenty feet from Clarence.

"Say, how's the fishing?" the man asked.

"Oh, with these big fat worms, I manage to catch a fair number," Clarence said.

"Let me see those giants!" the stranger said.

"Hey, come and see for yourself," Clarence insisted.

"Wow! They really are big giants. What do you feed them?" the stranger said.

"I usually feed them blood," Clarence said.

"Blood?" The stranger yelled.

"Yeah, I get cow's blood down at Mel's butcher shop in Prosper. How about you? Let's see your worms," Clarence asked.

"Wow! You got some really big worms there. What do you feed them?" Clarence asked.

"Two weeks ago, I gave them a real treat," the man said.

Just then the stranger reached into his bucket to fetch another worm. As he bent over, Clarence noticed that he had a mess of scars on his back. His shirt did not cover them enough.

"Say, I didn't get your name. My name is Clarence, what's yours?"

"My name is Caleb W. Henry," he said. Clarence's eyes popped!

"What does the 'W' stand for?" Clarence asked.

"It stands for Willard," Caleb said.

Clarence was stunned. "So, Caleb, where are you originally from?" Clarence asked.

"I spent my early years in Myrtle Beach, South Carolina. We moved here back in 1935. That's when my folks bought a farm just south of Prosper," Caleb said.

"Well, good luck with your fishing," Clarence said.

"I've already caught about eight fish. That will be enough for supper. I better get back to the farm and give my mother, Darla, a chance to clean them up," Caleb said.

Clarence stuck out his hand. Caleb reached out and shook it.

"Nice meeting you, Caleb," Clarence said. They both departed the fishing pond.

The Money Wars

Clarence vs. Betty

Betty came into the kitchen at the Hamley Farm. Clarence was just finishing up a bottle of whiskey.

"Clarence, I just came from town. Do you know what I heard from that banker, Percy Peters? He says that he is calling in our bank loan for the mortgages that we have been neglecting. All those loans are piling up and he wants to be paid. We are overextended everywhere. I thought that you were paying most of those bills. But you haven't! We owe money to the feed mill, the hardware store, the drug store, Mel's Meat Market, and even that handyman who fixed up the back porch. Everybody wants their money. What are you going to do about that mess?!" Betty yelled.

"Say, Betty, have you seen my brown belt?" Clarence slurred.

"Unbelievable! Everything does not revolve around you, you, you. This is serious stuff. The bank wants their money in thirty days, or we are out. We need money!" Betty said.

"Honey! Did I hear you say 'honey'? You haven't called me that in a long, long, time." Clarence slurred out.

Money! Clarence just did not worry about ready cash. He had some glass mason jars hidden in the woodshed. They were all filled with large bills. He had squirreled them away when he made the land sale for Bobby Joe's cash investment. At the end of the week, Betty caught Clarence while somewhat sober, only because he failed to buy a fresh bottle of whiskey from town.

"Clarence. Please listen to me. The bank is calling in all our loans. They are forcing us out. The only solution I can come up with is that my parents have a cottage over by Cape Girardeau. They are willing to let us live there until we get back on our feet. We need to go, and soon," Betty explained.

And so it was, Betty and Clarence packed up everything and moved to the cottage up in Sailor's Hill, Missouri on June 4th, 1941. Clarence appeared so eager to make that move, to Betty's surprise. Maybe the reality of their financial pressures finally made a mark on Clarence. Or the events of last month in Prosper or the disappearance of Bo Lukka that influenced Clarence's motivations.

In the years that followed, from 1941 to 1951, time became almost unbearable for Betty. Here she was, raising her only child, Farris, and taking care of a miserable drunk, Clarence.

Sailor's Hill, West of Cape Girardeau Missouri

"The Move"
1941

Two retired sailors from the U.S. Navy moved on top of this hill in 1910. They both spent about thirty years living in the two houses there. Thus, the name Sailor's Hill stuck. Jack Brandt, usually called Sailor Jack, was the man who had lived in what later became the Hamley homestead.

It was too bad that Sailor Jack departed this world so abruptly. He was killed when a sudden gust of wind blew down a heavy branch and crushed his skull without warning. His body was discovered at the bottom of his driveway. He was walking towards the mailbox. His brother, Lester, just stood there at the top of the hill and had a quiet moment, looking at his brother's dead body, then he turned his eyes to the sky.

"Yeah, it does look like it is going to be a sunny day. I think that I'll go back inside and celebrate with a bowl of cowboy stew."

Lester thought that Jack had been the most abusive person that had ever lived. Jack's former wife had thought the same, for she had left Jack about twelve years earlier.

Oh, but that's all gone now, the Hamley family now lives there.

To be sure, Clarence had brought his drinking problem with him from Wickers Wood. Even though he had his hidden money in those mason jars, that too was running thin. However, there was always that hidden bank account that nobody knew about. He had made a few extra thousand dollars from the sale of the farm back in Wickers Wood. He considered that his drinking money. Oh, if Betty only knew. He had a constellation of excuses to explain why all the money was gone, which only grew over all the years and yet so much of it led back to the drinking. But in 1951, the money train was gone. Somebody had to go to work.

Who was going to hire a drunk? Nobody. Clarence was not a very dependable worker. He wasn't even a dependable husband. Betty knew exactly what that meant for her. She was hired on as a home health worker for Dr. Bill Weston, who lived about a mile down the road towards Cape Girardeau. Every morning the good doctor would pick her up and bring her over to his house. Dr. Weston had an unwell brother that needed daily care. Betty became that caregiver.

One bright spot for Betty was her great fortune of having a good neighbor next door. That neighbor was Alice Ivers. The same could be said for Alice's 13-year-old son, Willie.

Willie was Farris's best friend. After school, they would spend time together. It seemed like wherever you saw one of them, the other was always nearby. Their favorite pastime was to race their scooters down their driveway – about three hundred feet – to the mailbox below. This race became a daily ritual for both of them during the spring, summer, and fall. Neither boy would ever forget one race in particular for the rest of their lives.

The Top of Sailor's Hill - Scooter!

September 15, 1951

"Come on Willie, let's give it a go!" Farris said as they both were set to race from the top of Sailor's Hill. At Sailor's Hill, there was a shared driveway that came together right in front of the Hamley house. Today, they were both ready to race their scooters as fast as they could. Their goal was to earn claim to the esteemed title, *King of the Hill.*

"So you think that today is the day that you can beat me to the bottom? Let's see who the first person will be to reach the mailbox," Farris said.

"I don't think so. I know so," Willie confidently assured his friend. Farris just smiled at Willie and thought for a moment – Willie is my best friend; I need to let him win something.

"Willie, I tell you what, the wheels on your scooter are small and my wheels are big. I'll give you a twenty second head start," Farris said as he drew a starting line in the dirt.

"Come on Willie, the wind is at our backs. We both should have a great run," Farris said.

Willie stepped up to the starting line and pushed off as hard as he could. He seemed to be sailing with a gust of wind at his back. His speed was too fast for any kind of control.

"Willie, you are going to fast! You might crash!" Farris yelled. To be sure, that is just what happened. Willie spun off the driveway and vanished into a bunch of tall pampas grasses. Farris stopped his scooter and quickly ran over to where Willie had crashed. Farris desperately waded through the tall grasses to find Willie.

"My God, are you okay?" Farris yelled with a crying voice.

"I'm okay! Everything is going to be just fine," Willie said with a smile on his face.

"How about the both of us take a little rest on that log over there," Farris suggested.

"Sure! Say Farris, look at the back wheel of my scooter. It looks like it's now wobbling," Willie said, looking worried.

Just then, a small tabby kitten came out from the pampas grasses and laid down by Willie's broken scooter.

"Say Farris, what do you make of that?" Willie asked.

"Oh, I think that kitten looks a little skinny. Maybe he needs some food," Farris said.

"Maybe he needs a good friend and a place to live," Willie asserted.

"I know, let's take him back to my place. Let's put him up in the woodshed. There is a hole in the back wall. He can come and go as he pleases," Farris said.

"That's a great idea, but what about your father? He is mean. What is he going to say?" Willie asked.

"We are just going to hide him for the time being. He doesn't have to know," Farris said, sounding like he was trying to convince himself.

On the way back to the woodshed, Willie turned to Farris and made a request.

"Farris, what should we call him? Every cat has to have a name," Willie said.

"I know, let's called him Scooter," Farris said. Willie agreed.

That evening, Farris waited for his father to fall asleep after his drinking spell. That is when Farris went out into the woodshed and fed Scooter some table scraps. As Farris approached the woodshed, he peeked though a hole in the door. On the other side of the door, he saw Willie feeding Scooter.

Once inside, Farris joined in on feeding Scooter the cat. Once Scooter was done, Farris made a plan.

"Say Willie, today is Monday. I'll feed him every Monday, Wednesday, and Friday. You feed him on Tuesdays, Thursdays, and Saturdays. We both can feed him on Sundays, okay? Farris requested.

"That's okay with me," Willie said. And that's the way it was from that day on.

Soon Saturday came and in from the back door came an old familiar face. It was Abraham Moses Victers, Alice's estranged husband, who came around twice a month. He would always arrive on a Saturday night, get all liquored up and spoiling for excitement.

As he came into the kitchen, there was Clarence polishing off the last of a bottle.

"Say Betty, reach into the bottom right-hand door of the sink and fetch that bottle of whiskey I've been meaning to sample. And make it snappy. Abe is here and he is dying of thirst."

Betty went and got the bottle and slammed it down on the table. From there she went and grabbed two shot glasses and poured them both a full shot, spilling some onto the table. Her hands were shaking.

Clarence grabbed her arm and pulled her close and then slapped her face. Her nose started to bleed. Blood dripped onto the floor.

"What happened?" Farris asked his mother.

"Oh, I slipped on some dish water by the sink and fell, bumping my nose."

Farris knew what had happened, but Betty insisted she had an accident. Farris retreated to his bedroom and waited until Abe left and Clarence had passed out in his bedroom while searching for his cigarettes.

Finally, it was about seven o'clock. Time for Scooter to be fed. Farris cut open a can of tuna and went out into the shed. Scooter quickly ate the entire can and then ran through the hole in the back of the shed. From there, he disappeared into the woods outside. This whole routine went on for about two weeks when all of the sudden there was no Scooter. He had been playing in the woods. Once Scooter came home, he was meowing at the back door. This got Clarence's attention.

"What is this? Why is this cat at our back door? Say, is anybody here feeding this beggar? Farris! Farris! Come over here. Do you know anything about this cat?" Clarence shouted at Farris.

"Oh, that's Scooter. He is an orphaned kitten," Farris answered. Clarence grabbed Farris by the shirt and pulled him closer.

"I thought that I told you more than once before that this house is not a barn for stray animals. You get rid of him or I'll do it my way. Got that? I am not going to start feeding this entire neighborhood. I am running out of money," Clarence said.

This was very true. Clarence was running out of money. He had spent his entire bundle on bad investments, binge drinking, and reckless spending. Now he was living off of Betty's money, which wasn't very much, once he cleaned out everything from the inheritance her parents left her. Every day, Clarence became more and more like the old Clovis that he once was.

The next day while Farris and Willie were riding on the school bus, Willie turned to Farris and said, "Farris, what's the matter? You don't talk today. Is there something wrong?" Willie said.

"It's my dad. Last night he was slapping mom around. Things never seem to change. Before I went out the door for school, mom said something strange. She said whatever happens, don't harden your heart. Promise me. She said that years ago a pastor named Bo Lukka said that in one of his sermons," Farris said.

All of the sudden, there was a fight on the school bus.

"I wonder what started the fight?" Willie asked Farris.

"Oh, that's just Floyd and Leon. They are half brothers. Half brothers always fight with each other," Farris said.

Willie's eyes started to open very wide. Farris could tell he was upset, but he continued to stare straight ahead as the bus moved towards school. Willie had a perfect reason to be worried. He had a secret in his head that he was not willing to share – especially with Farris.

That evening when Farris came home from school, he walked straight to the woodshed to check on Scooter, but the cat wasn't there. He checked everywhere and still there was no Scooter.

Soon around supper time, he was still checking around the house for Scooter. He started to smell a foul odor coming from the kitchen window, so he went inside the house.

Suddenly, Clarence yelled at him from the stove. Clarence was frying something that was quite grotesque.

"What's that on the stove?" Farris asked.

"Say hi to your old pal Scooter," Clarence said as he pulled Farris over to the table.

Clarence had skinned Scooter and fried him up on the stove and now he was trying to force feed him his loving pet.

"See! You made me do this. Stop your whining. This is all your fault. You made me do this. Maybe next time you will listen. I told you to get rid of that little beggar, but you wouldn't listen," Clarence said, full of emotion.

"You...you killed him. He...he...was my friend," Farris stuttered when he ran into his bedroom screaming as he slammed the door.

Back in the kitchen, Clarence grabbed his bottle of whiskey and took a large swig.

The very next day while Farris was sitting in his bus seat next to Willie he was very quiet, when suddenly he yelled out:

"I...I...hate him! I...I...hate him! My dad is the worst, and I...I...wish he was dead!" Farris yelled out with a stutter.

Willie and all the other kids on the bus could not believe what they were hearing. Everybody was completely shocked. All of the horror that went on in that kitchen produced a boy that developed a stutter.

At school, Farris' teacher became alarmed. She didn't know what to think. She talked to the principal about the problem and they both agreed that Farris needed help. Betty quickly agreed with the both of them and consented to admit Farris into a special needs class for one hour each day. The school nurse tried to find out how this whole thing developed, but Farris remained silent. He said nothing. He began to do what his mother had done. She suffered in silence for years. And that quietly became the habit of Farris.

One day on the bus Farris was silent as usual. He really didn't like to speak with the embarrassment of his stutter now plaguing him. But Willie, as expected, was curious mind.

"Farris, I haven't seen Scooter lately. I saw your father out by the shed yesterday. I wonder if he found Scooter. I hope not," Willie said, looking worried.

Clearly Willie did not know the truth about Scooter's death. Farris was not about to tell him. That was his secret.

"Oh...oh...I think that he ran off with some other cats. They do...do...that you...you...know," Farris stuttered out.

Secret! Farris was not the only one with a secret. Willie had a secret that he kept to himself for years. On one Friday evening in late September, Clarence hauled off and slugged Betty in the face for not accepting his advances. She received a black eye on the left side of her face. Monday was always laundry day. Betty and Alice had the habit of meeting out in the yard to hang the clothes on the line together while socializing. One day, Alice was turning her back away from Betty during their usual chores. Betty went over to her yard. Alice turned around and there on her face was a black eye on the same side of her face. Both of them just hung their heads in shame.

Alice knew exactly what had happened. Alice's estranged husband had been gone for about a week. Clarence had taken advantage of his absence and roughed up Alice for not receiving his advances.

"Betty, what are we going to do? I can't take this anymore," Alice tearfully said.

"I don't know, right now I have some housework to get done before Clarence gets back from the liquor store in Prosper. What am I going to do? I don't know. For now, I'm going to wait on the Lord. He will not disappoint!" Betty said.

Two days later, there was a truck accident in Arizona. Alice's husband was killed. The company that he worked for sent Alice an insurance settlement about thirty days later.

At Abe Moses' funeral, there weren't any people. Very few people could tolerate such a hell-raising person. But, what of Clarence? Both of them seemed to be cut from the same cloth. Perhaps it was...time for him to pay the check!

At the funeral, Alice stepped outside and had a brief conversation with Betty.

"Betty, this whole thing happened so suddenly without any warning," Alice said.

"So now what are you going to do?" Betty asked.

"I don't know. I think I will wait to hear from my sister. I sent her a letter this morning. She lives in Pennsylvania. Maybe she will have useful advice."

"You know Alice I often wondered, why do so many bad things happen to good people." Betty said.

"I wish I could answer that!" Alice replied.

"Maybe we are all sent here to this place called Earth because we are souls that need to be harvested," Betty said as she nodded her head in affirmation. She remembered what Bo Lukka preached.

For a brief moment both Betty and Alice just stood there and looked at each other's face.

"Clarence gave you that black eye, didn't he?" Betty asked.

Alice just hung her head and said, "I can't answer that."

"I know you can't. You wouldn't! You have always been someone just like me. You suffer in silence. That's why I have always thought of you as a great loving friend. God bless you, Alice," Betty said.

Towards the end of September 1951, the daily abuse of Clarence seemed to escalate out of control. That October 1st would change the Hamley's up on Sailor's Hill forever.

This day started out like most other days. Farris got up for school. He rode the bus both ways, like usual. When Farris and Willie came back from school, they stopped at the Hamley house and witnessed Clarence about to change a back tire on his Chevy. The car was positioned at the very edge of the top of the hill. To keep the car from rolling down the hill, he asked

Farris to bring him a board. Farris went over, got one, and placed it under the front tire to keep the car from rolling. In the meantime, before Clarence started the swap, he noticed that the mailman had just came by. Clarence walked down the hill to get the mail. He almost made it there, when the car rolled over the board and headed straight towards Clarence. The car flattened him out like a pancake. Farris could have warned him, but all he could do was stutter. Clarence was dead.

At the top of the hill Farris looked at Willie and said, "Everything is going to be just fine," with the vocal smoothness he once possessed.

The whole event was quite strange because the board should have held the car in place, but nobody would have guessed that all it would take is a sudden gust of wind to tip the front wheels over the board.

At the top of the hill, there they all stood. Farris, Willie, Alice, and Betty. They just stood there in a moment of silence, looking down at Clarence, the monster they knew him to be. The wind stopped.

Betty looked at Alice and expressed a few good words.

"Tomorrow, I'm going to spend the whole day emptying out whiskey bottles. My mind, body, and soul are completely exhausted," she remarked. Standing right next to Betty was her loving son, Farris.

"Mom, why did you stay? You should have left years ago," Farris asked. Betty's response was a defining moment for Farris.

"First, I had to keep promises. One for Sarah and one for my wedding vows. Second, I had no money, and I was married to a man that never wanted to work for us," she said, looking down the hill.

Farris stood there and looked out over the dead body of Clarence from the top of the hill and then raised his fist towards the heavens.

"Here is my promise," Farris said with conviction. "I will never be poor and true love will never be a stranger."

Twenty minutes later, Sherriff Edward Blake and his deputy Stony Frank arrived with the ambulance next to their car. The sheriff drove up the hill to the house to talk with Betty about the incident.

"What happened here?" Sherriff Blake asked.

"I don't know and I don't care. Ask my son, Farris. He was working with Clarence on the car," Betty said.

"Farris, could you please come over here. Tell me exactly what happened," Sherriff Blake asked.

"I killed him. I killed my dad," Farris said.

"How so?" Sheriff Blake said.

"I put the wrong size block under the front tire. It should have been larger," Farris said.

Sherriff Blake and Deputy Stony walked down the hill to view the body once again.

"Say Sheriff Blake, come over here. Look at all of those wounds on his back. It looks like he's had some beatings long ago. His entire back is a mess," Stony said.

"Yeah, no wonder he was such a miserable bastard. You know in the last two years we must have come out here to settle a disturbance at least ten times," Sherriff Blake said.

"Yeah, and every time Betty never once pressed charges. How could that go on for so long?" Stony said.

"Yeah, I hear you. Well, he sure paid the price for all his bad behaviour. Dead is a long time to be gone," Sherriff Blake said as he covered the dead body with a blanket.

Back at the house, the Sherriff spoke.

"You know Mrs. Hamley, I am going to take Farris down to the station. It would be best if you came along. I need to get a full statement about this whole matter. After all, Farris did say that he killed Clarence. I cannot ignore that statement," Sherriff Blake said.

Down at the Sherriff's office in Cape Girardeau, Blake brought in Betty and Farris. Standing in the doorway was the county attorney, Randy Biddle.

"Blake, what do you have?" Biddle asked.

"I've got a 15-year-old kid that says he killed his father, Clarence Hamley," Sherriff Blake said.

Biddle pulled Blake to the side.

"We are coming up to an election year. We've got to move fast on this case. Is that clear?" County Attorney Biddle said.

"Yes, sir!" Blake agreed.

"Okay, here is what I want you to do. First, we need to know if there was any bad blood between Farris and Clarence. Get a statement from his teacher, his school nurse, the principal and even his school bus driver. Get everything," Blake commanded.

Later on that afternoon, Attorney Biddle had all of his statements against Farris. Now there was a meeting in the county attorney's office. The attorney's office was filled with the school nurse, the sheriff, the sheriff's deputy, and of course, Betty and Farris. Biddle had the bus driver's statement laying on his desk.

Attorney Biddle read this statement to the group.

"Farris, these are your words, are they not? 'I wish my dad was dead!' Did you not say that on the school bus?" Biddle asked.

"I did!" Farris said. Everyone then became silent for a brief moment.

Then there was a loud knock on the office door. It was the front desk operator.

"Mr. Biddle, could I have a moment with you?" She asked.

"Well, there is another boy out here who says that he killed Clarence."

"What? Send him in." Biddle said. He came in.

"What is your name, son?" Biddle asked.

"My name is William Victor Ivers. Everybody calls me Willie. I did it. It was me!" Willie said. Willie wished to give himself up for his best friend.

Little did everyone know that just ten minutes earlier out in the parking lot, Willie overheard Deputy Stony's statement to a friend.

"Gee, it is really too bad about that kid Farris. Everybody at school says he was a great kid," said Deputy Stony sympathetically. "You know, if Farris were only 13-years-old, he would not end up in jail. He would only get some kind of counseling and then be released," Stony said.

Willie had heard everything, so he rushed into the sheriff's station and confessed to the killing. In his mind, it was very clear. Farris was his dear friend – a friend for life. But there was another reason. A reason that only his mother Alice knew about.

Willie was asked to wait out in the hallway while the county attorney wanted to discuss his case. Back inside the attorney's office, Farris was seated up next to Biddle. A paper was in Attorney Biddle's hands. It was a final statement about Farris' confession. He wanted Betty and Farris to read it over and for them both to sign it at the bottom.

As Biddle handed the paper over to Farris, the paper slipped out of his hands and drifted to the floor. As Farris picked up the paper, the shortness of his t-shirt exposed the belt marks on his back. Attorney Biddle saw it.

"Farris. I want you to lift up your t-shirt and turn around and face me," Biddle requested.

Farris did exactly as asked and then the entire room became very silent as they saw with their own eyes, the years and years of belt marks. There wasn't a dry eye in the room.

Finally, Attorney Biddle looked over at Captain Blake.

"This whole thing is going down as an accidental death. Deputy, please give Betty and her son a ride home. We…are…done…here," Biddle said.

And that appeared to be the end of all the sin, suffering, and death for Farris Hamley.

A few years later, County Attorney Randy Biddle was eating by himself in a restaurant. In came retired captain, Edward Blake.

"Say Edward, come over here and join me for lunch." They talked for about fifteen minutes during lunch, when Captain Blake asked Biddle a question.

"Say Randy, a few years ago when you had that Hamley case, I always wondered what were the reasons you dropped that case. Was it just the belt marks?" Edward asked.

"No! That was just part of the reason. For years, Farris had suffered in silence. He never told anybody at school or the police. He just took it with long suffering. Sometimes a person has to be a voice for those that don't have one. Every once in a while, a person has to step up and do the right thing, because it is the right thing to do," Randy said.

"Those are true words to live by. I was very glad to work under you. Randy, you are one of the good ones," Edward Blake said.

Both of them shook hands. Edward paid the bill and departed.

The following morning, back at Randy Biddle's house, there he was standing in front of the bathroom mirror, without a t-shirt. As he was shaving his face, he thought back to his memories.

"You know Randy, you can't save them all," he muttered to himself. After a long pause, he said with defiant determination, "No! But I can sure try! Remember what mother said she heard from that preacher man Bo Lukka – 'The earth is a place where souls are sent to be harvested'. I know the clock is ticking," he answered himself again.

If someone else was in the bathroom at this time, they would have noticed that Randy also had belt marks on his back.

Secret Bank Account

Now that Betty was the sole parent, her only option was to stay at her job with Dr. Weston. In some ways, it was unfortunate that the man who ran them close to bankruptcy was now dead. The bills were still outstanding and due.

Betty went down to the bank to learn about a loan. To her surprise, she found out that Clarence had a bank account, which she never knew about.

"Why, Mrs. Hamley, there is no need for such a loan. Your husband has an account with us. Here, let me check. Oh yes, here it is. It says that has an outstanding account for $8,700.00," the bank teller informed her.

Even with $8,700 in the bank, Betty was not about to quit her job. She knew that this money would not last forever. Anybody else would have cursed and hated Clarence, but not Betty, she had always been a forgiving person. This was true even on her most stressful days when Clarence was at his worst. He always made her work, work, work, and more work. He had to get even with women. His memories of Lusinda haunted him daily.

The Principal's Office

One day, Farris's teacher at school knocked on Principal Garret Tyler's office door. She was invited to come in.

"Mr. Tyler, I wish to speak to you about one of my students," she said.

"And whom might that be?" Garret Tyler asked.

"Farris Hamley, sir." Mrs. Pemble replied.

"What about Farris?" he asked.

"Mr. Tyler, Farris is in my 11th grade class. He is a gifted student. He has gotten nothing but A's in every subject. Sometimes I think that he could teach me," Mrs. Pemble said.

"So what's wrong with that?" Principal Tyler asked.

"Next year when he graduates, then what? He should have the opportunity to apply that gift he has – at a university or something. But that looks like it's not going to happen. He comes from a very poor family. What could we do? We should be doing something to make that happen," Mrs. Pemble urged her boss.

"I agree!" Principal Tyler said. For a moment, he sat there in silence. He looked over Farris's school records.

"You know, you are absolutely right, Mrs. Pemble. We need to do something. A mind is a terrible thing to go to waste. I'll tell you what, I'll speak to my brother-in-law about Farris. He is a professor at Princeton University. Maybe he will look into a scholarship." Principal Tyler said.

"You won't regret it." Mrs. Pemble said.

"Oh, Mrs. Pemble, don't get your hopes too high, but I'll see what I can do," he said.

A couple of weeks later, a defining moment of good fortune happened to Farris in his kitchen at home.

"Farris, Farris, could you come into the kitchen. I have a letter addressed to you. It is from Princeton University! Open it. Let's see what it says," Betty excitedly insisted. Farris did exactly that.

"Oh…my…God…I have been accepted to Princeton on a full scholarship!" Farris blurted.

"Farris, this is absolutely wonderful. I am so happy for you!" his mother gushed. "Sometimes good things happen when you wait on the Lord. He has a destiny for you, and I know it is a great one. With patience you will win your soul," Betty said with a smile.

By 1954, Farris graduated from high school. Everything was going well for him at this time except for one thing. Willie, his best friend, moved away about two years prior. Alice and Willie had packed up and moved away to a new life in Ohio. Understandably, this was a stressful event for Farris. He had lost his youthful years, most of which were bad, but the closeness he had with Willie would always remain.

Farris Moves Towards Big Money

From 1951 through the end of the 1960s, Farris concentrated on educating himself. He had gone through college, law school, and spent a couple of years as a tax attorney.

By 1962 to 1968, he had spent those years working for the law firm of Hamilton & Burns. While there, Farris felt like his aspirations exceeded his real expectations – he was underpaid.

In 1969, after being unemployed for almost a year, he packed his bags and headed for a change of scenery in Kansas City. After all, he did make that oath to God, that he would never be poor again and he hoped that Kansas City would be a place that protects this plan for him.

While in college, Farris learned how to play golf. Golf became one of his favorite pastimes. One day, he was playing the seventh hole of Grand Meadows Golf Course in Kansas City.

"I see that next shot of yours could be a problem," a fellow golfer remarked with a sympathetic voice.

"Yes, it does look rather difficult," Farris said. He got himself into position and made the shot very close to the intended hole.

"Great shot!" the golfer remarked.

"Thanks, I try to make every shot count," Farris declared.

"So, I've seen you out here at the course several times. You seem like a guy who knows what's going on. What's your name?" the man asked.

"Farris G. Hamley," Farris said.

"Well, how do you do, Mr. Farris G. Hamley? My name is Sid Vincent. You can just call me Sid," his new acquaintance said.

"It's a pleasure to meet you," Farris replied.

"So, Farris, what line of work are you in?" Sid asked.

"Oh, right now I'm unemployed. I have just spent the last six years working for a law firm called Hamilton & Burns. They gave me an office with a good title on the door, but when it came to money, they became very stingy," Farris said.

"I see, that could be a very bad problem," Sid said with a sympathetic voice.

"Yeah, money has always been a problem," Farris added.

"Just for my asking, what school did you go to and what was your major?" Sid asked.

"I graduated from Princeton with high honors. My major was Mathematics," Farris said.

"Numbers! I see. That's a great field," Sid exclaimed with raised brows, for Sid was also a numbers guy.

Farris stepped up to make his next shot, while Sid quietly considered Farris's employability potential with hopeful optimism.

"So, Farris, do you play the horses?" Sid asked.

"No, I don't know very much about horses," Farris answered.

"Well, I do. I make it my business to be on top of all the action. Tomorrow at noon, there is a horse out at Hollywood Turf Park; he's ready to win."

"I would like to help you out, being that you are unemployed. Here's a couple of yards ($200.00) take it down to the Club Lotus and talk to Freddy, the bartender. Tell him Sid sent you. He will place your bet to win on *Tango Turf* – the next 1st place winner in the second race.

Farris declined to take the money, so on the end of the last hole, Sid dropped the two hundred dollars into Farris's golf bag and departed. Sid was very pleased with himself. He thought that his money would do all the talking. Farris saw him make the drop and he took the bait.

When Farris got back to his apartment, he removed the money and came to the decision that, well, he has nothing to lose in the matter. That night he went down to the Club Lotus and found Freddy, who waved him over to the bar.

"Say Farris, your ship just came in. Here are your winnings." Freddy handed Farris six hundred dollars in large bills and a free drink.

Over on the side of the bar were two people. One was Sid Vincent and the other was Rudy Paul, the owner of Club Lotus. Sid came over and congratulated Farris on his winnings.

"Farris, why don't you take that money and buy yourself some new threads. I think you would look real good in something more stylish. Get your new clothes and meet me here tomorrow night at seven o'clock. I know someone who could use a man that had a good business sense about him. I guarantee it will be well worth your while. You do like money, don't you?" Sid asked hypothetically.

Farris gave Sid his phone number and left the bar. When he got home, he thought over the entire offer and rationalized that some money was better than no money. *I'll do only what I was trained to do and nothing more,* he thought.

Ten minutes after Farris got home he received a phone call. It was Sid.

"Say Farris, I called to tell you that when you come into the club tomorrow, tell the two doormen, Mr. Smith and Mr. Jones, that you are here to see Rudy. They will escort you over to the correct booth," Sid said before he hung up the phone.

The next evening, Farris approached the doormen at Club Lotus.

"Well Mr. Smith. I am here to see Rudy," Farris said.

"I'm not Mr. Smith. Tonight, I'm Mr. Jones. I was Mr. Smith last night," the doorman replied, curiously.

"I see, well, tell Rudy I am here to talk," Farris said.

One of the doormen took Farris over to the correct booth. As Farris sat down at the booth, he said, "Gee, these two doormen are as big as monsters. You must have an expensive food bill just feeding them," Farris said to Rudy.

"Oh, it's not the food bill that worries me," Rudy said, looking over at the burly man walking away. "It's the rabies shots that are killing me. Every now and then, one of them goes off the rails. He begins to toss a rowdy customer around like a rag doll, if you know what I mean. It costs me big money just to bail 'em out of jail. Sometimes I have to go to the mattress for some extra cash just so I can make that happen. It's expensive, but it's the cost of doing business. Mr. Smith and Mr. Jones keep the riffraff out of my club. That way, I can give my good paying customers the peace of mind, just so you know," Rudy said.

"I must say, you do have a very nice night club, Mr. Paul," Farris said.

"Thank you. It's nice to hear some gratitude once in a while. Now, let's get down to business. Sid tells me that you might be somebody that I might be interested in. Sid does have a great eye for talent."

Mr. Paul stared at Sid, who appeared to know right away what that meant – *hook him up.*

"So, Farris, Sid tells me that you are good with numbers," Paul said.

"Yes, that was my major in college. I majored in Math," Farris told the man.

Paul gave Sid another long stare.

"So, listen Farris, as soon as Sid checks you out, I'll put you on the payroll," Paul said.

"That would be great Mr. Paul," Farris remarked with a sense of surprise.

"It's Pauly, you can call me Pauly, okay?"

"Sure thing, Pauly," Farris said.

Pauly got up from his seat. The meeting was over. Pauly slammed a hundred–dollar bill down on the table and said, "Sid, see that our new employee gets everything that he wants for dinner. It's on me."

Pauly nodded at Sid, motioning him to accompany him to the night club entrance door. Once there, Pauly grabbed Sid by the arm and exchanged a few words.

"Sid, I want you to check this guy out. I want to know everything about him. If he spits on the sidewalk, I want to know. If he has an overdue library book, I want to know. Got that?"

"Yes, consider it done," Sid said.

Pauly left the club. Then, Sid waved with his finger for Annie, the waitress, to come over to the door, which she did immediately.

"Yes, what is it, Sid?" she asked.

"Annie, I want you to make friends with that guy over in that booth. His name is Farris Hamley. Find out what he is all about. Get him to open up. If he has any flaws, find them. Pauly wants to know, and you know Pauly – he wants results," Sid said to Annie.

"Sure Sid. I'll do my best. I'll do whatever it takes," Annie said.

"That's what I like to hear," Sid said with a smile.

Annie went back to Farris' booth

"So what's your pleasure tonight?" She handed Farris a menu as she bent over and met face-to-face. At this moment, they both looked straight into each other's eyes.

"What's my pleasure? I would be a fool if I said 'not you'. You look great! What is your name?" Farris inquired.

"Lisa, my name is Lisa Ann. Most people just call me Lisa. Only people that I think I would like to know usually call me Annie. You can call me Annie," she said with a smile.

"That's great! I want to be on your good side," Farris said as coolly as possible.

"My good side? I would just like you to be on my side, period," Annie said.

By now, Farris was flattered beyond all expectations. As Annie turned to leave the table she said, "I think your friend, Sid, is coming back from the men's room. I'll take your order then okay?" Annie said. As Annie finished up with the menu order, she dropped a note in front of Farris. It said *call me.*

Farris took her phone number and stuffed it into his jacket. When he got back to his apartment later that is what he did. He called her. That phone call produced not one, but several dates. Annie was always pressing Farris for personal information about his life.

On their fourth date, there they were in bed together for the first time. After they made love they both just laid there staring at the ceiling and began talking.

"Say Annie, I notice a small scar by your left eye. How did you get that?" Farris asked.

"Oh, it was my dad, he slugged me when I spilled one of his drinks. He was a mean drunk," Annie said.

"Well, he had better not do that again or he'll answer to me," Farris said.

"You won't have to worry about that too much," Annie said with assurance.

"How so?" Farris asked.

"Well, Pauly sat down with him one day and had a serious discussion. The next day, dad moved to Atlanta. He must have liked it because he never wrote or came back. That was two years ago. I have been working for Pauly ever since."

"And Farris, tell me about you. How do you feel about life? Tell me about Farris Hamley," she asked.

"Well, there isn't much to tell that is very pleasant. I was born in Wickers Wood, Missouri. We lived on a farm. And when I was 15 years old, we moved to Sailor's Hill outside of Girardeau. My father was a drunk and my mother was a saint. She put me through Princeton University and then law school. We were always poor, and my father always blamed my mother and me for all his bad choices. I think that he was a person with a dark past. I once made an oath to God that I would never be poor and despised by others as long as I lived," Farris explained.

"You know what? We have had similar lives. Somehow, I feel very close to you Farris," Annie said.

"So, we have a lot in common? I feel the same, Annie. You are the best thing that has ever happened to me," Farris said.

Immediately, Annie felt guilty. Here she was trying to squeeze information out of somebody that was like herself. By now, she had fallen for the guy. She was in love. This whole thing was not supposed to happen, but it did.

For once in her life, Annie had started to have thoughts about a future with a man she loved – Farris Hamley. She also had made an oath with God. Her oath was always in the back of her mind. She wanted to marry a loving husband, buy a house with a white picket fence, and have several happy children. She wanted everything to be just normal. But how could she convince Farris? Big money was soon coming into view. Was it going to be a blessing or a curse?

Once Annie had come back to work at Club Lotus, Sid approached her and motioned her over to a booth.

"Now Annie, I want to hear some good news. Tell me about this guy, Farris. What are his faults? Where are his weaknesses?" Sid questioned Annie.

"Money, he is into security. He told me that he never wanted to be poor again. That's it!" Annie said.

"So, it's money. We can take care of that. Good work, Annie. I knew I could count on you. There will be some extra cash in your envelope this week. You earned it," Sid said.

By 1970, Farris had been working for Club Lotus for a year. His financial situation had greatly improved. He was still busy bookkeeping for Pauly. But little did he know that Sidney was busy maintaining a second set of illegal books for Club Lotus. All of the inventories were false. The money was rolling in.

In late September, Farris proposed marriage to Annie. She was delighted. She said yes! With some secret help from Pauly, Farris purchased a home with a white picket fence, on the west side of Kansas City. Things now appeared to be working out according to hopes and plans for Farris and Annie.

By summer of 1973, Annie was working part time at Club Lotus and Farris, well, he never stopped working. Their home on the west side of town had become a business office for Pauly and Sid. One of them was always there talking business. Annie soon had her fill of the whole situation.

On one occasion, Annie found herself finally alone. She was sitting on her back porch, reclined on a lawn chair. The sun was warming her face. Her mind drifted back to her honeymoon at Lake Tahoe – the swimming pool, the warm sun, the simple companionship of her lover, Farris. Everything seemed like it was a lifetime ago.

As Annie was sitting there, soaking up the warmth of the sun, Farris came over and sat down in a lawn chair beside her. She immediately got up and walked away. She wanted to show contempt for her lifestyle. Her home was nothing more than a business office to her.

Farris sat down on the empty chair and started to let the sun warm his face. While sitting there, his mind drifted back to an earlier time when his mother had warned him about the love of money. Her words were clear inside his head.

Farris, what does it profit a man if he gains the wealth of the entire world, and on his last day, he loses his soul? Those words started to haunt him. This became a time to reflect, and it wasn't going away. But was it too late to save his marriage?

Dangerous Money

1974

Back inside the house the phone rang. Annie took the call and beckoned Farris over to the phone.

"Farris, this is Pauly. I need to have a sit-down with you. I need to clear up a few loose ends. Meet me down at our office warehouse on 5ᵗʰ Street at seven o'clock. Come through the back door. A doorman, Mr. Jones, will open up after four knocks, okay?" Pauly instructed.

At seven o'clock, Farris arrived. As expected, he knocked four times and Mr. Jones opened up. Farris walked in and went directly to Pauly's office.

"Farris, sit down. There are a few things that need to be said. First, I want you to know that I trust you with my life. These last couple of years, you have been my right-hand man. Sid is a loyal soldier, but you...you are the one I trust the most. Out in the shop there is a row of lockers. Most of them have tools in them, but there is one that is always locked. Here is the key. It's the only one that exists. Inside the locked box is a stack of papers and a bag of cash for emergencies. Now, in three weeks, I am having a meeting with some Colombians about a business deal. If anything happens to me, you've got the key. I want you to have it," Paul said as he shook Farris' hand.

Before Farris could walk out the door, Pauly called him back.

"Say Farris, I know that you and Annie have been working a little too much. That kind of stress can put too much anger into a marriage. I tell you what. How about the both of you take a Hawaiian cruise. It's on me. It will give you some free time to just lay back and put your feet up and let somebody else do the worrying. I'll call you later when you get back home. In the meantime, ask Annie if she is up for something like that," Pauly said.

"Sure enough, I'll expect your call," Farris said.

In the meantime, Sid made a business call to Pauly.

"Say Pauly," Sid said.

"This is Mr. Benson," Pauly lied. "Who's calling? Let me guess, it's you Sid. Are you calling on our office phone?" Pauly asked.

"Yes!" Sid replied.

"How many times have I told you. All my calls that you make are to come on a public phone," Pauly scolded Sid.

"But this is important!" Sid said.

"What is it?" Pauly asked.

"Have you noticed that Annie is getting a little testy lately? She might take Farris away from our business," Sid said.

"Listen and listen good. The problem has already been solved. Now hang up the damn phone," Pauly insisted.

"Okay Pauly," Sid said.

"Once again, that idiot calls me over our business phone..." Pauly ranted to himself. "Why do I pay that guy the big bucks? Why?" Pauly rolled his eyes while thinking about Sid's judgement.

The next day, he wasted no time in calling Farris back.

"Say Farris, put Annie on the phone," Pauly instructed. She came to the phone.

"What is it?" Annie asked.

"Say Annie, I've got some good news for you both. Both of you have been working too hard. It's been work, work, work. It's time to take a break, so you can get your head clear. Look, everybody understands that. So, here's what I propose. How about taking a nice Hawaiian cruise? It's all on me. I'll pay for it. What do you say? It'll have good music, good food, island hopping – all fun. How about it?" Pauly asked.

"Yes, yes, yes! I am ready right now!" Annie exclaimed.

"Great! Put all your beach clothes together. Tomorrow you go, okay?" Pauly said.

"Could you put Farris back on the line? Just for a few seconds," Pauly asked.

"Sure!" Annie replied excitedly, thinking about their spontaneous getaway.

"Say Farris, earlier I gave you that key, I hope that you keep it in a safe place," Pauly said.

"I do. It is in my safety deposit box at the bank," he replied.

"Great! Now, there is another matter that I need to talk about. Let's meet tonight for supper at Geno's Restaurant at six-fifteen, okay?

There they were, Pauly and Farris, sitting at a table for two, over in the corner of the restaurant.

"Farris, remember that real estate contract I had you sign. The one that is in the tool locker. Well, just so you know, that contract makes you the sole owner of some great beach property in Maui. I had to use your name for the contract because my credit was too bad. But this can become a win-win for the both of us. A lot depends on a group of investors back in New York. I know for a fact that they will have their eyes on that property. If anything, ever happens to me, call a guy named Riff in New York. His private number is in the tool locker. Believe me! They will be more than willing to part with twenty million for that real estate. That's what my inside info has told me," Pauly said.

"Glad we talked. Pauly, I've got your back," Farris said, as the meeting came to an end.

"I know you do. You are the one guy that I can trust," Pauly said.

They both shook hands and started to depart.

"Oh, Farris, I almost forgot, here are your airline tickets for San Francisco. The flight is for tomorrow at one. By seven tomorrow night, you should be boarding your airplane for Hawaii. Have a great trip," Pauly said as he handed Farris all of the tickets.

"Oh, and Farris, don't worry about anything. All of your arrangements have been made. Just enjoy!" Pauly insisted.

The next day, February 10th, 1974 came fast. Farris and Annie flew out to San Francisco. The vacation turned out to be more than they expected. They both flew out and took a cruise ship back. It became a defining experience for both of them – one that would change their lives forever.

Farris and Annie both enjoyed island hopping in Hawaii, all the entertainment, the village shopping, the food, the music. Finally, after two weeks of fun in the sun, there they were, just one hour from docking at San Francisco's Pier 17 to end their cruise. Annie approached the cruise director on the top deck.

"Hello, excuse me, my name is Annie, could you please tell me when the ship is going to dock?" Annie asked.

"My best estimate is about forty-five minutes," said Director Ida Reed.

"Thank you," she responded.

Annie's View from the Cruise Ship's Top Deck

Annie sat down at a table with Farris on the top deck of the cruise ship.

"Annie, I'm going over to the bar and get us a drink. I'll be back shortly," Farris said.

Within three minutes, he had a drink for each of them.

"I have got to go to the bathroom," Farris said. He left the table and went down to the open deck below. From the table, Annie could see most of the area. As she was looking, she noticed Farris had stopped to talk to a familiar face. It was none other than Sid Vincent.

"Oh my God, that bastard! All this time we were supposed to be on a fun vacation, and here he was... This was nothing but a business deal! This is never going to change. I feel like everything was a big fat lie!" Annie yelled out loud. People around her thought that she had lost it with her rage. In truth, Farris didn't even know that Sid was onboard the ship.

For a brief moment, Annie just sat there and stared at those two drinks. With her left hand, she tipped over Farris' drink onto the table. She stood up and collected her emotions.

"So that's the way it's gonna be," she said to herself.

Once Farris came back to the table, Annie looked at the spilled drink and made a remark.

"Well, it looks like a mistake was made," she said.

"Things happen," he replied.

"Farris, we need to go back to our room and finish packing our luggage for our departure," Annie remarked.

Later, as they both departed the ship, Annie turned to Farris and said, "Farris, I need to go into some of those gift shops for a gift souvenir."

"So do I," Farris said with a smile. "Let's meet back at this same spot about thirty minutes from now. That should be enough time for the both of us," Farris suggested.

Annie and Farris went into different shops. When Farris was buried in a shopping line, Annie disappeared. She headed for a public phone booth that was visible nearby. She made a call to an old friend that lived in San Francisco.

"Hello, Mickey, is that you?" Annie asked.

"Yes, who is calling?" Mickey asked.

"This is Annie. You remember a few years ago when you told me that if I ever needed a favor, you would help?" Annie said.

"Oh Annie! How have you need been? I missed your sweet smile."

"Mickey, I don't have much time. Could you come down to Pier 17? I desperately need a ride," Annie pleaded.

"Why, sure! I live only about ten minutes away. See you soon. Oh! Annie, what are you wearing – so I'll be able to find you?" Mickey asked.

"Look for a pink dress and a sun hat," Annie said.

"I am on the way," Mickey replied.

Mickey made it down to the pier in about eight minutes. Annie slipped into a shadow behind a car and disappeared.

While Mickey and Annie were going back to his apartment, Annie made a short confession, "Mickey, I am leaving my husband. I have reached a boiling point with that man," Annie said.

"What happened?" Mickey asked, surprised.

"I think that I've just become another business deal. It all makes sense to me now. I once asked him about his life. His response was that he'd never be poor again." Annie looked far off out the car window, eyes welling up with angry tears. "So my response now is 'Go find your pot of gold!'" she choked out with resentment.

Annie left Mickey's apartment and refused to say where she was going.

Back at the gift shop, Farris looked every place. He could not find Annie, so he called the police. A squad car came down to service the call.

Out of the squad car stepped Sergeant Taylor.

"So let me get this straight Mr. Hamley. You and your wife, Annie, went on a Hawaiian cruise. You both came back and did some shopping, and now your wife is missing. Have you and your wife been having marital problems lately? When was the exact last time you saw her?" Sergeant Taylor asked.

"My answer is no! We have not had any problems and the last time I saw her was right here in this shop," Farris said, irritated.

"Mr. Hamley, you are going to have to come with me down to the station and make out a missing person's report. Please get in the squad car," Sergeant Taylor requested.

Down at the station, the missing person's case was given to Lt. Saunders. He took down Farris' statement and so, the next day, Lt. Saunders put together a fact sheet.

The same day, Farris came into the office with a piece of paper in his hand. It was a note that he found inside his suitcase.

Farris, I hope you find what you are looking for. I once thought that it was me. It is kind of strange, the value people place on money. I hope that it doesn't ruin your life. It's not going to ruin mine. Goodbye, Annie.

At this time, Annie did not yet know that on this vacation she had become pregnant.

After reading Annie's note, Lt. Saunders was worried. His thought went against Farris. He could have written this note. Could they even get a sample of Annie's handwriting? Maybe.

After forty-eight hours, the missing person's case was now in FBI jurisdiction. Farris was told to go back to Kansas City. The FBI was going to handle it from here on.

The Hamley case was handed over to Special Agent Dan Lockner, who paid a visit to Captain Scott Dillard in the police department. Into the office came Lt. Saunders with a paper in his hand. It was a fact sheet on Farris Hamley. S.A. Lockner looked very surprised.

"What is going on here? I thought that this was a FBI case. Are you guys going to dig around and upset everything? You guys just want Farris Hamley to be good for this murder. We want him on multiple federal crimes. Stay out of it. Let us handle it." S.A. Lockner demanded.

Around the San Francisco police station, the word was that Farris Hamley had gotten away with murder.

However, the district attorney could not find some valid reason to pursue the case. He lacked probable cause, witnesses, there was certainly no body, and Farris' life insurance policy named Annie as the single beneficiary.

Both the police and the FBI dropped the case, but suspicion was there. Was this the last time the police would ever question Farris' innocence? Maybe.

Once Farris arrived back home to Kansas City, Sidney welcomed him back, despite his knowledge of the mishap on the vacation.

Farris arrived at his west side home and Sidney's second call gave him a real reason to worry.

Farris told him how bad his trip was, saying, "Annie left me. She's gone. In her note, she said she is not coming back," Farris said with a broken voice full of emotion.

"This is bad. This is real bad. Pauly has got to know. I'm going to tell him tonight at our meeting," Sid couldn't wait, so he called Pauly up on the phone. Five minutes later, Pauly called Farris.

"So, I hear that you and the Mrs. had a little tiff," Pauly tried to minimize it.

"It was more than a little tiff. She's gone!" Farris exclaimed.

"I see. So she's really gone. Is that going to be a problem for me?" Pauly asked.

"No!" Farris said.

"So how much did you tell her about our business. I gotta know. I don't like loose ends," Pauly said.

"Nothing, she knows nothing," Farris said.

"Good, that's what I like to hear," Pauly said.

Later on, Farris called up Sid and asked him if Annie was going to be safe.

"Sid, this is Farris. How is Pauly taking all the changes?" Farris asked.

"Farris, you know Pauly, anything can happen. Make sure you make it to that special meeting tonight, down at the 2nd Avenue warehouse. Be there at eight o'clock sharp. This is a very important meeting. Pauly has a guest coming from Colombia. A major business deal is in the mix. Be there!" Sid insisted.

Farris hung up the phone and started thinking to himself.

A big business deal! What kind of a business deal are they talking about? What do I have to do with that? I'm just an accountant. I don't do business deals.

With his insistence, all of Pauly's employees were to attend, including the Club Lotus doormen, Mr. Jones and Mr. Smith. That, obviously, was not their real names, of course. Sid, Farris, and Pauly were all going to be there. Finally, the meeting time approached. Farris showed up five minutes late. As he approached the warehouse, there was a sudden explosion. It was so massive that Farris didn't exit his car. The heat was too great.

Soon, as the fire became intense, the fire department arrived, and four fire trucks put the flames out. The fire marshal, Steven Stikes, was on the scene when it reached containment. S.A. Lockner came over and greeted his old college roommate, Steven.

"Well, what brings the FBI out to this fire, Dan?" Steven asked.

"Oh, we have a vested interest in this fire. We were forewarned that some very bad Colombians were here. These were very bad criminals."

"Just so you know Dan, our fire team found a roulette wheel in the back room, along with a large card table. The Colombians? And now, it looks like their welcome has expired. No IDs here," Steven said.

On the sidelines was Farris Hamley. As he walked back to his car, his mind raced with thoughts about the incident and its implications.

I guess I won't have to worry about Annie getting killed by Pauly. At least she's now safe. Once he got back to his car, he just sat there and tried to formulate his next step.

"What am I gonna do? Oh, what am I gonna do?" he muttered amidst his stress. *The tool locker, the tool locker…I've got to get over to the main office on 5th Street and remove all those documents. But wait, you need a key. Gotta get my key before the authorities find everything.* Farris was now on the run.

The very next morning, he was the first customer at the bank. He got his key and drove over to the 5th Street office. Immediately, he removed everything from the tool locker. It was a duffle bag filled with cash and the mortgage contract for the Hawaiian property. Within five minutes from the time he left the warehouse, the FBI arrived to begin their search. This was a very close call for Farris.

On the way back to his west side home of Kansas City, he attempted some rational thinking. He thought about the huge sum of money. Perhaps it belonged to business associates out east in New York. And that mortgage – it was paid in full. How could I let that go, he thought. *It's in my name. What would that group of investors do...now that they had to deal with me? I need a plan, and fast.* His panic mode was working overtime.

Farris, think, think, think. He quickly formulated an escape plan that he was satisfied with. *I'll get a room outside of town. I'll dye my hair, then I'll fly to Chicago. From there, I'll drive to Minnesota. I'll use the cash and not leave a paper trail to follow. That's it!* From St. Paul, he drove all the way to the west coast.

The day after the warehouse fire, S.A. Lockner talked to Steven Stikes, the fire marshal.

"Steven, how does this all look?" Lockner asked.

"Dan, somebody didn't want those people inside the warehouse to get out the back door. The back door was blocked with an old junk car. They must have drove it right up to the door and pulled the keys and left," Steven said.

Three days later, Farris was in a motel on the outside of Los Angeles. Los Angeles became his town. He figured that the population and the climate suited him just fine.

Since everybody at the warehouse in Kansas City had been unexpectedly cremated by the flames, personal identification was impossible to confirm. Farris was hoping that he would be listed as a possible victim. For a very long time, Farris lived under the radar because he used nothing but cash for all his transactions – money that was from the old tool locker. He kept looking over his shoulder for some mobster to show up, but it never happened. As far as the police were concerned, it was just another cold case to be filed away at their warehouse.

One full year had passed since Annie left. Farris's dream of spending his entire life with Annie were now gone. Spending every day just doing nothing but existing was a miserable life not for him. He decided to turn inward and pursue his second love. The love that was expressed in his oath to God. Security! Was this going to replace, Annie, his beautiful first love? Even when his motivation was less than perfect, he still knew how to make money – and lots of it!

Being that Farris had ownership of that Hawaiian beach front property, he decided to go into the real estate business, at least for the time being.

As the years flew by, Farris had the big success of flipping houses for huge profits.

Sale of Beachfront Property

June 1980

In 1980, Farris made his way to Hawaii. He had the sale of all that precious beachfront property on his mind. Into his office came a businessman. He was wearing a Hawaiian shirt decorated with palm trees. In his right hand, he was carrying a brief case.

As he sat down in front of Farris, he remarked, "Mr. Farris G. Hamley. So…we finally meet. My name is Riff Marteen and I am from New York." He could see a bit of tension appear on Farris's face upon his introduction and he swooped in to quell the concern.

"Relax! This is only a business talk. Nothing personal. Me and a number of businessmen in New York are all interested in that beachfront property that you are holding. We are well-prepared to make you a reasonable offer. I'm sure it will be one you cannot refuse, so let's get down to business. You know what they say – time is money," Riff said.

"What I have in my hand is a certified bank check for twenty million dollars – yours in exchange for all of your beach property. And that must include those properties that you recently purchased, which are on both sides of the main property. Do you understand? I'm sure that my offer is quite reasonable," Riff continued.

That's when Farris put both hands at the top of his head and slowly slid them down over his face. He looked up into Riff's face and stared.

"You know, Riff! I...am...tired. I am really tired of looking over my shoulders. Somehow, in the back of my mind, I always knew that you people would show up. And here you are! So let's get it over with. Where do I sign?" Farris asked.

Riff removed the documents from his brief case and handed Farris the check. There was a silence in the room for a minute or so, then Riff spoke up.

"You know Farris, you were pretty hard to find," Riff said.

"Yeah, for years I paid cash for everything. I never left a paper trail," Farris said.

"That is what I would have done. Farris, just between you, and me, and the lamp post, I was never going to do you any physical harm. There are no businessmen out in New York. Today, it is only me. Over the years, most of them died of old age or they were eliminated by their infighting. That kind of behaviour is really dumb. Dumb is dead, and dead is a long time to be gone. Farris, I am curious, with all of your money, why do you live in such a modest house?" Riff asked.

"Riff, when I was very young, my mother taught me that...people are more important than things," Farris said.

"Now that sounds just like *my* mother. When I was a young man, she used to tell me about some preacher man down in Missouri, who expressed those same thoughts. It seemed like every other day she would hit me with one of his quotes. I think that she wanted me to become a preacher or something. Can you see me as a preacher? I think that I have too much of a fondness for large sums of money. I hope that I never have to choose between kindness and money. That would be such a great test. Yeah, mom would say something like that," Riff expressed to Farris.

"Farris, once I found you, I did some checking on you. From what I've got from others, is that you are a stand-up guy. I like dealing with a stand-up guy. You see, in my line of work, most of my business associates barely qualify as human beings. It's a real pleasure to see somebody like you. You must have been raised by kind parents," Riff said.

"Mr. Marteen, I can only say that you are half right. It was my mother that set me straight," Farris said.

"Your mother! I knew we had something in common. Say Farris, don't tell anybody that I said that. I don't want people to think that I'm going soft or something," Riff said, as he departed.

Farris and Willie Reunite

September 1991

Sooner or later, it had to happen. On a late September night, while Farris was burning the midnight oil working late, Trudy, his secretary, received a call from the main lobby of the FGH Building on the first floor.

"Trudy, this is Lyle at the main desk. There is a gentleman down here that would like to see Farris. Do me a favor, ask him if he wants to see him at this late hour," Lyle said.

"Lyle, ask the gentleman what his name is." A minute passed by.

"Trudy, he wouldn't say, but he said 'scooter,'" Lyle said. Trudy told Farris and without delay Farris asked Trudy to send him in.

Willie came up to the tenth floor and exited the elevator. From there, he was directed to go down the hallway. Farris's office door was open. The man stopped at the doorway for thirty seconds. The hallway light behind him produced a shadow of a man, dressed with a hat and briefcase.

Farris turned around in his chair and paused for a moment and stared at the figure.

"Willie, is that you?" Farris asked.

"Well, I don't go by that name anymore, but you are right. It's me! Today, I go by the name Victor W. Reed."

"Oh, Willie, you will always be Willie to me. Come in and sit down. I want to know everything. Where have you been?" Farris asked.

"As you know, back in 1954, me and my mother moved to Ohio. Soon my mother left me and then I was placed into a temporary home. Those folks were very nice to me. We soon became a full-time family. They adopted me and I took on their last name as my own. Today, I am a retired school principal."

Willie continued, "Back in 1974, I got married to another schoolteacher. Her name was Marie. Two years later we had a daughter, named Ida. A few years ago, my wife Marie passed away from cancer. Ida married a navy man. Now she lives in San Francisco," Willie said.

"So what line of work does she do?" Farris asked.

"She works on some cruise ship. She really enjoys her work." Willie said.

"And you? How do you fill your days?" Farris asked.

"Being retired is not for wimps. I try to keep myself busy with social clubs," Willie said.

"Willie, why don't you make yourself busy right here. You can work in this building. Work for me. It's the least I can do? After all, you are the best friend that I ever had," Farris said.

"Farris, I don't know much about your work. I wouldn't fit in here," Willie said.

"Fit in? You will fit in if I say so. And I say so. Willie, I will teach you everything that you need to know. I insist!" Farris added.

It did not take long. Willie came into work a few days later and he saw a name plate over an office door. It read, Victor W. Reed, CEO. Farris had soon turned

Willie into a quick study. He involved Willie into every business transaction that he could.

Over a period of about eighteen months, everybody who worked in the offices of Farris G. Hamley had become one big, close family. All of the employees loved their jobs. Before long, Willie became the go-to man. That got a lot of things done. For Farris, finding Willie was an unexpected joy.

Farris and the New Scooter

1992

About one year later, while sitting in that same window chair that he always sat in, Farris noticed one large gray rain cloud outside. Today was his walk day. He was planning on going down to Vic's Restaurant for a noon lunch. Trudy, his secretary, just announced that she was leaving for her lunch hour.

"Mr. Hamley, is there anything that I can get you before I leave?" Trudy asked.

"Oh yes, it looks like rain. Could you find my raincoat?" Farris said. Farris got his raincoat, put it on, and left his office. Farris walked down to Vic's restaurant and sat on a bench outside the entrance. Suddenly, along came a brown, tabby coloured kitten. He laid down on Farris's foot. Farris reached down and picked him up and started to pet the kitten.

"Ohhh, there you go. That's a good boy. I am glad that you finally came back. I have greatly missed you Scooter. You haven't changed a bit. You are the same old Scooter," Farris said.

Farris stayed there for about fifteen minutes. All the time, he was looking for the owner, but nobody showed up, so he stuffed Scooter into his raincoat and went back to the FGH Building.

When Trudy came back from her lunch, she heard Farris talking in his office. She peeked around the open door and saw Farris sitting in front of his window, overlooking the city.

Trudy noticed something different. As he sat there, he was petting a kitten and softly talking.

"There you go, Scooter. You can stay here with me. You will be safe from that bad old man. He'll never find you here," Farris said gently.

Trudy just smiled, for she herself was a kind of pet owner. For her, this was a good thing. From that day on, it became a daily routine for Farris to sit in front of his window and pet Scooter. Scooter got his own room in the FGH Building.

Even though this kitten was not the original Scooter, Farris felt like it was. This became one of his defining moments – finding an old-time friend.

The Shepherd Counseling Agency and Detective Bernie Smithe

December 1999

With Willie here and Scooter back again, Farris had only one missing love. And that love was *Annie.* Where was she, his long-lost wife? Based on her goodbye letter, he didn't expect to see her again.

For the last twenty-five years, Farris accepted the fact that Annie was planning on starting over with somebody else. And now, saturated with enormous wealth, he had a wealth that preserved his security, but lacked joy.

Oh, if joy could only come back to greet me, I would pledge to offer up two sacred words: I'm sorry. Farris sat in his window chair daily and whispered those words to himself.

Farris wanted help, but he didn't know where to start. Trudy, yes Trudy, she will help me. She has been my loyal secretary for eight years. She is more than an employee; she is my friend. And that is where he went for help. Farris dumped his feelings onto Trudy, and she felt flattered. Trudy was quick to make arrangements for Farris to get counseling, so she called up the *Shepherd Counseling Agency* and made an appointment for Farris to see a counselor. That counselor was both the owner and therapist, Bob Shepherd, who was a former minister before entering the world of counseling. It was December 3rd, 1999. When Farris arrived at the clinic, he was greeted at the door by the owner, Mr. Shepherd.

"Come in, come in, I am Bob Shepherd. I will be meeting with you. Come with me to my office. Straight down the hallway. That's it, come in and have a seat."

"Now, Mr. Hamley, may I call you Farris?" Bob asked.

"Yes, please do." Farris answered.

"So, Farris tell me about yourself and then let's talk about why you are here, okay?" Bob said.

Farris went through his childhood at Sailor's Hill, his marriage to Annie, and her disappearance. And then, his wealth.

"Farris, most people that I talk to are usually plagued with a lot of pain. That's a given. Tell me about something good that happened in your life. Let's start there and see where it leads," Bob suggested.

"Good?! The only thing that I embraced from my childhood was the unconditional love that my mother and I shared together. My guess is, that I expected that same love from my wife, Annie, but that just did not happen. She left me for good," Farris said with a weakened voice.

"Farris, might I ask, what is it that you do for a living?" Bob asked.

"Since 1991, I have been running FGH Corporation, which is a corporation that subsidizes low-income housing and small businesses," Farris explained.

"That seems like a good endeavor," Bob said.

"I guess so!" Farris said.

"Farris, from what I have heard you say, you seem like a man that lives with a purpose. You are somebody that is purpose driven. Most people that come into my office lack that quality. You are to be commended for that," which Bob said was a great quality to embrace.

"Bob, I have worked very hard over this last decade. And yet, I feel so empty. Money itself has not made me happy. The one thing that really haunts me is that I don't know what happened to my wife, Annie. I need to know if she is happy, or even alive. I got to know!" Farris said.

"Farris, being that you have the wealth that you do, you could easily find her if that's the case, but you should be discrete. Don't jeopardize her happiness."

"Farris there is one thing that I want you to realize," Bob said. "What's that?" Farris asked.

"Farris, this world is not our playground. Souls were sent here to Earth to be harvested. Try to embrace that and you will do well," Bob said.

"I get it." Farris said as he got up and ended his counseling session.

Before he left the room, Farris turned back and looked at Bob, who stood up from his chair and spoke a few words of encouragement.

"Farris, with patience you will win your soul." Farris nodded with affirmation and then left the building.

Later that day, Farris came back to that same building on Western Avenue and stood at the front door. It was locked. Suddenly, a man came up to the front door with some keys in his hand.

"And how can I help you, sir?" the man asked Farris.

"My name is Farris Hamley. I am here to make another appointment for next week," Farris said.

"Appointment! This is a property that is owned by the California Builders Association. Nobody has done any business here since 1941. I am a custodian. Somebody called me and said there was a person down here inside the office, so I came to check on things."

"You come down to check on things? Let me tell you something. This morning I sat in that office straight ahead and had a counseling session with a man named Bob Shepherd. That happened," Farris insisted.

"Not possible! This property is vacant. It's scheduled for demolition next week. Here, I'll even open the front door and let you see for yourself." They both walked inside.

"My meeting was in that office straight ahead," Farris said. They both walked through the open office door.

The custodian looked at Farris quizzically.

"See, there is nothing but dust and a broken window behind the desk and chairs. Are we done here?" the custodian asked.

Suddenly a breeze came through the broken window and forced the office door to close. Behind that door was a dusty picture of a man sitting at his desk. At the bottom of the picture there was a name. It said, Bob Shepherd, December 3rd, 1941.

Farris was speechless and confounded. He returned to his office at the FGH Building. As he sat in his window chair with Scooter on his lap, he whispered to himself.

"What was that? What now? What am I gonna do? Annie! I've got to find Annie," Farris said to himself.

Trudy came into his office and put a stack of new papers on his desk. These were not just ordinary papers; they were names and addresses of people that were seeking small business loans for new start-up businesses in and around the city of Los Angeles. Everyday, he received a new stack of files to work on. The SBA sent him the names and Farris shelled out the cash for start-up expenses and building mortgages. Around the offices in the building, he became known as a sort of socialist Santa Claus.

The Smithe Detective Agency

December 4th, 1999

Farris was in need of some help. He called Trudy, his trusted secretary, into his office.

"Trudy, could you do me a favor? I need the help of a real good detective agency. Could you get a phone number and set up an appointment as soon as possible?" Farris asked.

One day later, a gentleman from the *Smithe Detective Agency* was in the lobby.

"Mr. Hamley, there is somebody out here that wishes to speak to you," Trudy said over the intercom.

"Send him in," Farris replied.

"Hello, my name is Bernie Smithe. I am here to answer to your call."

"Come in, come in, Mr. Smithe," Farris said.

"It is my understanding that you wish to find someone. Is that the case?" Bernie asked.

"Yes, it's my wife. She has been missing for about twenty-five years. She left me back in 1974. I want you to find her and report back to me," Farris said.

"Ah, Mr. Hamley, we are a five star detective agency. Finding somebody that doesn't want to be found can become very costly, given the time it can take," Bernie said.

"Cost?! I don't care what it costs — just find her," Farris demanded.

"Okay, I like to discuss right up front, as it is a part of the service. If I put my head-hunting squad on this case, it will cost you about a thousand dollars per day, plus expenses. It is high, but these guys get results," Bernie said.

"Good, just do it," Farris insisted.

"Tell me, Mr. Hamley, did Annie have any relatives that she spoke of?" Bernie asked.

"Yes, sometimes she spoke about her sister. Her name was Inga Wright. She lived in Chicago. Maybe she still does. I don't know," Farris said.

"We will find out. I'll check with you in about a week, if that's okay." Bernie said, as he left Farris's office.

One week later, Bernie came back.

"Mr. Hamley, I've got some news for you," Bernie said.

"Just give me the bad news first, and then the good news," Farris said.

"Mr. Hamley, it is not good or bad news. It is just news. We found her. She is alive and well. Her sister Inga still lives in Chicago. She told my detectives that Annie moved to Grand Rapids, Michigan in 1974."

"While living in Grand Rapids, she married and had one son in 1975. Today, she still lives there in an assisted living apartment. Her son is a practicing attorney," Bernie said.

"I see, well you have done your job as I had asked, Mr. Smithe," Farris said.

"But, don't you want to know her last name and phone number?" Bernie asked.

"No! Here is an envelope with a check for seven thousand, plus a bonus of an additional three thousand for your quick service. That will be all Mr. Smithe," Farris said as he handed him the money.

Bernie left the office satisfied.

The Bribe

June 2000

Between 1975 and 1991, Farris Hamley had accumulated close to two billion dollars. However, since 1991, when the FGH Corporation was founded, he had been depleting his asset pool just helping people.

Never did he ever do something that was under the table until now. Even that was not for personal financial gain.

A new development started in the summer of 2000, a year that was flawed.

It was June 10th, 2000 at the Roosevelt Golf Course in Los Angeles. Out on the seventh hole, was the district attorney, Marshall Mason. Arriving at the same hole at the same time was Farris Hamley, an acquaintance of Mason's.

"So, Marshall, I heard that you are up for retirement later next year. Is that true?" Farris asked.

"No. It will be earlier than later. I've got about twelve months to go and then I'm done," Marshall stated.

"After retirement, what's next?" Farris asked.

"Me and the Mrs. are looking at property up at Lake Tahoe. We both have taken trips up there and are now looking to buy a house," Marshall answered.

"Any house in particular?" Farris asked.

"Funny you mention it, yes. My wife is in love with a home on, I think it's Pine Ridge Road. 1700 Pine

Ridge Road, I believe. It's going to break her heart when I tell her that we cannot afford it," Marshall said.

"Oh, that's too bad. Maybe something good will happen. Surprises do happen," Farris said.

"Yeah, but buying that house would be a little out of my league. They want almost three million dollars for that homestead. I just didn't have the heart to tell my wife yet. Maybe next week," Marshall said.

They both finished playing golf together and agreed to meet and play together the following week.

One week later, there they were out on the fourth hole, when Farris turned to Marshall.

"You know your last drive came very close to that hole. It looks like you might have a problem with the next shot. There is a small mound in front of the hole," Farris said.

"Oh, I'll deal with that when I reach the hole," Marshall said. While walking down the fairway, Farris changed the subject.

"Marshall, you know I took a look at the property at Lake Tahoe. I thought about it for three seconds and then, I decided to buy it outright. I paid three million dollars on the spot. I now own that property. I tell you what, there is an up-and-coming attorney – I think that you work with him. His name is William G. Hawkins. If you were to put him on your short list for your next replacement, somebody like myself might sell you that property for one tenth the price, but you got to make that next shot to close the deal," Farris said.

Marshall looked at Farris with a very sober face. In his mind, the stakes were very high. He thought about his wife and her wishes and his peace of mind.

He approached the fifth hole and studied the shot for almost two minutes.

"Well, I guess it's now crunch time," Marshall said. He made the shot from ten feet away. A week later, Marshall and his wife moved into their retirement home at Lake Tahoe. Farris had already made the arrangements.

The newspaper article in one of the early editions quoted Marshall Burk as endorsing William G. Hawkins as his replacement for the Los Angeles District Attorney.

Farris, Marshall, and William were all pleased with the changes.

Vanity O' Vanity

D.A. Hawkins Settles In
November 2002

On his first day in his new office, District Attorney Hawkins was eager to establish some new habits. Every time he entered his office, he would walk over to his favorite wall with all of his awards and degrees and straighten the picture of himself holding his law degree. Everyday, it seemed like it was a little off center, so he straightened it.

Then, at exactly ten in the morning he would have his coffee while seated in his chair by the window, which to his pleasure, had a nice view. Little did he know, on the other side of town, Farris Hamley was also drinking his morning coffee with a friend in his lap – Scooter.

At this point in his life, William Hawkins had an optimistic point of view with a glorious future ahead, but vanity was his curse. *Vanity o' vanity... thy curse has become thy shame.*

On November 16th, temptation showed its face. As William sat there in his morning coffee chair in front of his picture window, the office intercom became alive.

"Mr. Hawkins, there is a Mr. Chester Finch from Barrister & Finch Builders Association. He would like to speak to you. May I send him in?" Kindra, the secretary said.

"Yes, please do," William said.

"Hello, Mr. Hawkins, my name is Chester Finch," Finch said.

"Mr. Finch, how may I help you?" William asked.

"It is nice to meet you, Mr. Hawkins. I'll get right to the point. Mr. Hawkins, I represent a group of investors that share a vision for the northwest side of Los Angeles. Our research indicates that there is a viable market there for a high-end shopping mall. However, we seemed to be stalled by the city's preoccupation with the Girrard Company, who has a plan in place for some money-sucking, low-end housing project on the south side. That project is spearheaded by a Mr. Farris Hamley," Finch explained.

"Our sources have told us that this Farris Hamley has bought five city counsel votes that are ready to okay this pork barrel project. What most people don't know is that this Farris Hamley has a criminal past. Did you know that he once worked for a criminal organization back in Kansas City? He worked at Club Lotus – a known hangout for mobsters. And there is more, he is also believed to be responsible for the murder of his wife, for which, he never spent one day in jail. Who could ever trust an animal like that?" Finch continued.

"Farris Hamley is laughing at the criminal justice system for the city of Los Angeles. We would like to know, sir, is that okay with you?" Chester Finch said, finishing his monologue.

"Let me assure you, Mr. Finch, if we ever come up with some solid evidence, this office will not hesitate to put him behind bars," William said.

"That is certainly good to hear, Mr. Hawkins. It certainly feels like you are a team player. I think that we both want the same thing then. Oh, and just so you know, if this criminal does find himself behind bars, that would put you, Mr. Hawkins, in a very good position in the next upcoming election. A number of our very important people would show their appreciation, even if you were to run for governor," Chester Finch said.

"I'll see where the evidence leads me," D.A. Hawkins said, as the two shook hands. Chester Finch walked towards the door.

"Mr. Hawkins, our city council is still stalled with this housing project. Our investors in the mega mall are still waiting for some good news," Mr. Finch said as he was leaving.

The Whistleblower

December 2002

On June 2nd, 2002, the previous D.A. Marshall Mason, left a stack of cold case papers on his desk. Unfortunately, two months later, that same stack was still there.

In the meantime, another case was about to take center stage. It was the Girrard Company. They began to lay the cement foundations for the south side housing project.

The Girrard Company began their building project in early June 2002. Halfway through the cement pouring, an anonymous caller phoned the local newspaper, claiming he had a blockbuster story for sale. He accused the Girrard Company of using cheap imported cement and rebar. This was in violation of the building code for the city of Los Angeles.

The building project was about to come to a halt. The city counsel was now undecided as to whether they should go ahead with the housing project. Everything was now in limbo.

It did not take very long to put Farris G. Hamley up on the front page of the local paper. Why? Girrard Company was owned by Farris, so he got all of the blame for bad management. Farris had put the entire project into the trusted hands of a leading member of the board of directors, Clayton Burrows.

Clay Burrows overbilled the entire operation and sent huge profits to Riff Marteen in New York.

D.A. Hawkins did not have these facts. He just pursued that man with all the headlines – Farris Hamley.

Eventually, his whistleblower witness, a man by the name of Jason Zauler, came forward and went to the district attorney's office for some confirmation as a state's witness against Farris Hamley.

Inside the D.A.'s office, Hawkins said that he was going to put Zauler and Burrows up on the stand as a witness for the prosecution. Zauler knew about Burrows' connection to the mob boss in New York, so he fled the D.A.'s office in fear of his life. Zauler then went underground and disappeared for about six months.

Clayton Burrows was in panic mode, because he was the one who gave the okay for the Girrard purchases. In his panic, Clay Burrows made a desperate call to Riff Marteen, his underworld boss back in New York City on the morning of December 4th, 2002.

"Say Artie, put Riff on the phone. I need to have some serious words with him," Clay said.

"Clay, what's up?" Riff asked.

"Riff, we have a problem. Jason Zauler, one of our employees at the Girrard Company, is spilling his guts to the L.A. District Attorney about our building materials. That's not all of it. Jason split – he's gone underground. I can't find him. Things are becoming unraveled," Clay said.

"Clay, calm down. Here is what I want you to do. Find him and take care of the situation quietly. Reach into your rainy-day fund and put some serious cash into his pocket. Money talks! Oh, and Clay, there is no 'we' in this problem. You fix it and don't call me again about 'your problem,'" Riff said as he slammed the cell phone down to the floor and squashed it with his foot.

Clay went back to his office at the FGH Building. Once there, he thought about the whole situation. Clearly, there could be no case for D.A. Hawkins as long as there was no whistleblower, but where was Jason?

Six months had passed by and finally there was Jason. He was spotted by Clay at the Bayport Restaurant near Long Beach. Clay and his girlfriend happened to be dining there at the same time.

Once Jason and his date finished their meal and left the restaurant, Clay followed him back to Jason's girlfriend's house in Gardina, a suburb of L.A.

Clay returned to his office at the FGH Building and called up Mannie Kane – a known hit man with a big reputation. By doing this, Clay broke protocol. Clearly, his instructions were stated by Riff – resolve the problem quickly and quietly with a handsome payoff. Clay was a wizard with numbers, but when it came to 'people problems', he lacked good judgement.

There were some things that Clayton did not know and some things he should have been made aware of. Things that did not need to escalate to murder. For example, the Federal Trade Commission had gotten their nose into the substandard building case against the Girrard Company. They were just about to issue a large fine on FGH's owner, Farris Hamley. He had already agreed to pay the large fine. He then fired the entire board of directors at Girrard Company. This action satisfied the federal investigators, but here comes Clayton Burrows, trying to solve a problem that has already been solved. Clay was just not plugged into reality.

The Girrard case was brought to a close, but that still left the attempted murder case against Farris Hamley as an open case. D.A. Hawkins was not about to let that fade away. After all, there was a police shooting involved with Mannie Kane. And then, there was that note written by Farris Hamley.

Once again, things started to heat up. Police Lt. Lawson and D.A. Hawkins were assembling their case. December 4th, 2002 was a very busy day for D.A. Hawkins. Perhaps things were going to get better once he got home for dinner.

The Hit

December 5th, 2002

Jason Zauler was at his girlfriend's house in Gardina, California. He was standing by the mailbox near the street. Suddenly, there was a speeding car approaching him. Behind the wheel of that car was Mannie Kane, there to eliminate the whistleblower. To be sure, Mannie had a bad rap sheet with the police.

Mannie's car struck Jason, who flew into the air. On his way down, his arm hit the side of a tree, causing a fracture. Jason survived the hit and was taken to the hospital after the incident.

It was too bad for Mannie, there was a cop car only one block away at the time. Soon, the chase was on. And why not? Mannie zoomed right past the patrol car as he headed for the freeway. This chase went on for about one mile, when Mannie's car hit the guard rail. Mannie got out of his car and tried to make a run for it. He turned around and shot at the cops twice, they returned the fire and killed him.

Afterwards, Lieutenant Lawson went over to the body of Mannie and searched him for identification. In Mannie's back pocket, he found a note written on a memo pad from the office of Farris G. Hamley. His own personal letterhead was displayed on the top of the note.

Lt. Lawson read the note.

Eliminate that talking parrot A.S.A.P.
                                    -Farris

Lt. Lawson urgently called D.A. Hawkins.

"Mr. Hawkins, I've got some real news for you. You might want to come down here and see this for yourself. We are only about two miles from your office. I'll have a patrol car bring you down to this scene. We just killed that psycho hitman, Mannie Kane. He had in his possession a memo note from Farris Hamley. You've got to see this," Lt. Lawson said.

"Fantastic! I'll be right there," Hawkins responded.

Once Hawkins arrived at the scene, Lt. Lawson handed him the memo note.

"Great! You've done good work, Lawson. I'll see that this all gets put into your personal file," Hawkins said.

Lt. Lawson offered to give Hawkins a ride back to the office. On the way back to Hawkins' office, Lt. Lawson made an unwanted remark.

"You know Mr. Hawkins, this whole thing is a little too easy. Things just don't add up. How does a billionaire like Farris Hamley write such an incriminating note like that? That memo note reads like something a high school dropout would write. This just doesn't smell right. There has got to be more to this crime," Lt. Lawson said.

"Lt. Lawson, don't be taken in. You are starting to sound like my wife. She'll see the good in everyone," Hawkins said.

"As a policeman, I have got to let the actual evidence lead me where I need to be. However, if everything becomes too easy, I gotta tell you, I need to dig deeper. It keeps me honest," Lt. Lawson said.

"Lieutenant Lawson, do you think that I am honest?" D.A. Hawkins asked.

"Yes, I do!" Lt. Lawson answered.

On the drive back, nothing else was said. Silence filled the car. This conversation about being objective and honest was not over, for in his office, his wife, Lora, was about to clarify their home life. In the office, William's talk began.

"Lora, this conversation will just have to wait until I get home for supper. We will talk then," William Hawkins said as he picked up the phone for another call. Lora left his office, with her usual frown.

After Lora left the office, Hawkins took that note and sat down in his window chair. While there, he recalled that recent conversation with Lt. Lawson, who's words rang true. *Follow the evidence, see where it leads, dig deeper! Keep yourself honest,* Hawkins thought.

No matter how much he wanted to close this case, Lt. Lawson was right, so he gave in. Yes, Hawkins needed to be on the straight and narrow. He quickly called Lt. Lawson back into his office for a consult.

"Lt. Lawson, I see that this note is on a corporate note pad. I want you to find out if everybody else in that FGH Building uses this same memo pad or has access to the Farris Hamley memo pads. Check all of their waste baskets and see if anybody uses this paper. If you have to, talk to the janitor. See if he has thrown out this week's trash. If he hasn't, get it. Bring it here," D.A. Hawkins said. Lt. Lawson's investigation began.

Dinner Argument: William vs. Lora

December 6ᵗʰ, 2002.

By the morning of December 6ᵗʰ, 2002, everything seemed to be escalating out of control. This would become a very, very busy day. First, there was Jason Zauler, who at nine o'clock in the morning, had a cast put on his broken arm. A short time later, he exited the hospital for reasons unknown.

By eleven, D.A. Hawkins called the hospital, only to find out that Jason had left unexpectedly. Hawkins flew into a rage. He headed for the FGH Building to question Farris.

At noon, D.A. Hawkins arrived at the FGH Building. As the elevator door opened, William ran straight forward. He stopped for about a few seconds and shouted at Trudy, the secretary.

"Okay, where is he? Where is Farris?" William shouted.

"He's in that office straight ahead," Trudy said as she pointed, looking confused with the commotion.

Once inside Farris' office, William continued his rage.

"Okay Farris, where did you stuff him? Where did you stuff Jason Zauler? I want to know right now. I'm going to charge you with obstruction of justice, and I can make it stick," Hawkins demanded.

"What are you talking about?" Farris asked.

"I see, that's how you are going to play it – the dumb act. This dumb act has saved you many times before, but not today! Just so you know, the police department is on to you. You've got one foot inside a jail cell and the other foot resting on a banana peel. Don't make any long-term vacation plans. I will be back with a warrant for your arrest, just as soon as I talk with Judge Burger. I'll see you later today," D.A. Hawkins said as he left the building and headed back to his office.

Once he arrived there, he had some bad news. The judge was on vacation. William wanted to work with Judge Burger because he had been liberal in his decisions that benefitted the police.

D.A. Hawkins was still in a bad mood, so just to set things straight he called Lt. Lawson into his office.

"Lt. Lawson, I want you to keep a tail on this Farris guy. Watch him, see where he goes. See who he meets. I want to know everything. He just might do something cute, like skip town. You never know how these money bags think! Be ready for the unexpected," William warned.

"Yes sir, I'll get right on it," Lt. Lawson said as he left for the FGH Building. Before he got there, Trudy had a few precious words to share with Farris about the angry rage that William had expressed.

"Farris, don't pay any attention to what D.A. Hawkins said. I know you. You are a very kind and generous person. There are not many people that would spend their entire fortune on people in real need. Some day will come when he will apologize," Trudy said.

"I hope so, I really hope so," Farris said.

"I hope that happens," Trudy said.

"You know Trudy, most people see their own truth; these truths are sometimes based on a false sense of assumptions. We all do that. Just look at how people used to believe the world was flat. They really believed they were right. I trust that the good Lord will straighten this whole mess out," Farris said.

December 6th was indeed a very bad day for D.A. William Hawkins. Maybe things were going to get better once he retired for the day, had a pleasant dinner with his wife and Lannie, his daughter.

Oh, but things were about to escalate to a higher level of clarity. There they were, William and Lora, facing off in the kitchen at home. The talk was about having a better understanding about feelings and quality time together.

"William, I came to your workplace today at noon. I wanted to have a surprise lunch with you, but you were not there. As I looked around your office, I noticed your big mess. What is going on with you? There were pizza boxes stacked up in corners. Every chair had stacks of papers. Your desk is covered with coffee stains. The walls were covered with post-it notes. Where is all this crazy behaviour coming from?" Lora asked.

"I know, I know, it's this cold case with Farris Hamley and the connection with another current case I am working on. I think everything is connected. Ever since I opened up that cold case, there has been nothing but phone calls from all over. This case might be the biggest one of my career. Just the other day, there was a Mr. Chester Finch of the Builders Association who suggested that if I solve this case, I might have a good shot at the governor's job in the next election," William said.

"Oh, now I understand, this is all about you, you, you. I just want to know where I fit in, where your daughter fits in," she said with disgust.

"At what point to do we start to have a normal family?" Lora questioned.

Just then the phone rang. William picked up the receiver. He looked at Lora.

"We will have to talk about this later," William said to Lora, who threw her hands up in response.

That night just before supper, the house phone rang, and Lora took the call. It was for William Hawkins.

"Not again! I don't believe it. This is our family time," she said, as she dropped the receiver to the floor. William picked up the receiver off the floor and took one more message about the now infamous Farris Hamley — a favorite subject for him.

When Williams was done with the phone call, Lora cornered him in the kitchen.

"William, my minute is here. I need to say something. Something that you need to hear," Lora said.

"What is that?" William asked.

"William, if a person spends most of his time looking for all the bad in life, he will find it. If you spend most of your time looking for the good, you will find that also. Wouldn't it be wiser to have some moderation? Not everything is all black or white. There are some shades of gray. This Farris thing that you have might have some shades of gray. You know, you might be wrong about the whole thing! I remember when we first got married, you said something that I never forgot," Lora said.

"What was that?" William asked.

"You...said that the Earth is a place where souls are sent to be harvested. Didn't you?" Lora said.

"I guess so," William responded.

"Well, if that's so, shouldn't we live with grace for grace?" Lora questioned.

"Oh, now you are starting to sound like my mother..." William said.

"If she was all wrong, then I want you to look me in the face and say so," Lora demanded.

William looked down, avoiding her eye contact.

"I thought so!" Lora said.

"Lora, it is my job to look at all of the evidence and see where it leads me," William said.

"That seems fair enough. Just don't come to a conclusion before you even get started," she added.

After this brief interaction, they sat down and ate together as a family. This daily tiff was beginning to take its toll. Lora was determined to keep the discussion about Farris Hamley to a bare minimum. It was clear to her that William had a strong obsession with locking up Farris. What Lora didn't know was his motive. Was William just doing his job or was Chester Finch going to get his way?

The Hospital: Riff's Last Confession with Father Romono

December 7ᵗʰ, 2002

"I bet you a steak dinner that my sister Sophie sent you, didn't she? Well, I'm not dead yet, so come on in and view what's left of my personality," Riff boasted. Father Romono went over and closed the door.

"Riff, I am here to offer you a chance to come clean with the Lord. This could be your final hour. You need to confess your sins while you still can," Father Romono said.

"Don't bother, there is no hope for somebody like me. I know what I am," Riff said.

"Riff, the good Lord is merciful. He stands at the door waiting for your knock he saves with grace," Father Romono said.

"You know, you are starting to sound like my mother. With her, there is always hope. My mother, she was always like a saint or something. She never had an evil thought in her heart. God bless her soul," Riff spoke softly.

"It sounds like you really loved her. Tell me about your family life with her," Father Romono asked.

"Well, she wasn't religious. She was more like a person that had some kind of personal relationship with the Lord. I always felt guilty around her because she was so kind. I think she got that way when she was younger. She once told me that she grew up in some small town in Missouri. I can't think of the name of that town. Maybe it will come to me later," Riff said.

"And your father. What was he like?" Father Romono asked.

"He was a little too practical. He never seemed to know how to bend or go with the flow," Riff said.

"Riff, what was your main issue with your father?" Father Romono asked.

"There was this one time, when he was laid off work, I offered him a percentage of my take on some hot items. He got mad and ordered me out of the house. What's with that? Try to help somebody and all they do is push you away. I was just trying to be a helping hand and he just gave me a lot of grief," Riff explained.

"My father, Charles, wasn't the only one who didn't appreciate a helping hand. My sister, Sophie, and her boyfriend didn't have any wheels to take her to the prom. Me, being the thoughtful person that I am, boosted a car for him. I was only going to keep it until the prom was over with and return it. It was our neighbor's car. He didn't need it for one day. Besides, he got it back one day later with a full tank of gas. Sophie told my dad and, once again, he tossed me out of the house. What's with that? They both treated me like I was something stuck to the bottom of their shoe. People! Try to help them....You would think there would be some sort of gratitude," Riff said with a sarcastic told.

"I can remember way back when… my friend, Zak, gave me a great tip on a winning horse. It turned out to be a lot of cash in my pocket. I showed my gratitude. When he said that he needed a new television, I got him a new one. So, what if it was hot? It's the thought that counts! Isn't it?" Riff said.

Father Romono just rolled his eyes.

"Riff, I'm sure that there are a lot more serious things that you should confess. Isn't there?" Father Romono asked.

"Yeah, I suppose there is. My mother once told me to never be the reason for someone else's sin, suffering, and death. I tried my best to make that true. Sure, I've taken a lot of bribes, kickbacks, and payoffs, but I never put the hit on someone, and I never wiped them out, money wise," Riff said.

"Your mother sounded like a very kind person," Father Romono said.

"She was. It's kind of funny how a person thinks when he has so little time left to live. I start to remember all the little things that I took for granted. Now, suddenly, they are big things. They are things that made me who I am," Riff explained.

"When I close my eyes, I can see my mother and me sitting at the kitchen table. She used to talk about her earlier days when she used to live in Missouri," Riff continued.

"What was it like for her?" Father Romono asked.

"Oh, she talked about living in a small town. I think it was called Prosper. The town had one gas pump, one grocery store, a small park, and a one room church. By today's standards, it would be called a one-horse town and that town died. But you know what, sometimes big is not better. The people there were all one big family. Family! Isn't that everything? My mother used to say, people are more important than things. Was she wrong?" Riff asked.

"No Riff! She got it right," Father Romono said.

"Father Romono, as long as I'm giving my confession, could you come closer, so nobody else can hear. That's close enough. Okay, years ago there was a rumor going around that I put a hit on Rudy Paul in Kansas City, back in 1974. Just between you and me and the lamp post, it wasn't me. I only took credit for it, but it was somebody else. It was that psycho Mannie Kane or some FBI guy by the name of Lockner. My money would be on Lockner. My information on him was quite clear. He was a demolition expert in the U.S. military. Kane, well! He couldn't organize a Kool Aid stand. I took credit for the hit because it put me in a better business position. People in high places finally took notice. The money opportunities came my way, but there was a drawback." Riff said.

"What was that?" Father Romono asked.

"When a guy gets big and noticed, he becomes powerful. That power can lead to many worries – like jealousy and envy. There is always somebody waiting to take your place. I am sick and tired of looking over my shoulder…if you know what I mean. When a person gets old, he wants to have some peace of mind. Is that asking too much?" Riff asked Father Romono.

"You know, Riff, peace of mind, means many different things to many different people," Father Romono said.

"Well, to me Father, it means waking up in the morning and not finding yourself 'D' as in dead!" Riff said.

Riff's Miracle

December 7th - 9th, 2002

The phone call came in at about nine o'clock in the morning on December 7th. It was Judge Burger's secretary.

"Mr. Hawkins, our office received your message and I wanted to tell you that Judge Burger will be back in at eleven today. He is scheduled to hear only one case – at two," the secretary said.

"Finally!" William Hawkins said with relief.

"Is there some additional message that you want me to give him?" she asked.

"I'll call him at eleven fifteen, if that's okay," William said.

Meanwhile, twenty past nine, back at the New York University Hospital in room 112, there was a doctor and his assistant giving Riff Marteen a gloomy prognosis.

Drs. Berg and Pantino stood bedside and briefly looked at their clipboards for Riff.

"You two guys look like a couple of morticians. How about taking your business elsewhere," Riff chuckled?

"Riff, this looks serious. Your G.F.R. reading is 30." Dr. Berg said.

"Okay, what kind of moon man talk is that? Can you two lab coats speak plain English?" Riff asked.

"Okay, in plain English, this means that your kidneys are failing. You are going to need a kidney. For that, you need to get on the transplant list immediately or you will be strapped to a machine for the rest of your life," Dr. Berg said.

"Okay, now tell me the bad news," Riff said.

"The bad news is that we need to find a viable kidney," Dr. Berg said. Both of the doctors excused themselves and left the room.

Across the country in Los Angeles, there were some interesting developments. Coming down the hallway in the FGH Building were two co-workers and associates – Farris Hamley and Clayton Burrows. They both were on their way to the lunchroom to rescue some coffee and doughnuts.

"Clay, you look a little worried today. What's the matter?" Farris asked.

"Oh, it's a friend of mine back in New York. I just heard that his kidneys are failing. There might not be any donors," Clay said.

"What hospital is he in?" Farris asked.

"He is in the university hospital," Clay said.

"Well, that is a really sad story to hear. I will pray for him," Farris said.

Farris got his coffee and doughnut and went back to his window chair in his office. He sat there and thought for a couple of minutes. He thought about that warrant for his arrest. He could feel his face turn hot.

They must be on their way. I need to get out of here and very quickly. I need to go now! Farris took the elevator down to the basement, where there was a connecting hallway to the next building. Within minutes, he was gone.

By now, things were about to happen at the D.A.'s office. William got his warrant and by lunch time he was there in the FGH Building. He was there to spoil Farris's lunch and arrest him. But where was he? He stormed into the office lobby.

"Okay, where is he?" William demanded an answer from Trudy.

"He went to lunch," Trudy said.

"Oh, where is that?" William asked.

"That's straight down the hallway. You will see it when you get there," Trudy said.

"That's okay. I can wait!" William said, with a grin.

D.A. Hawkins did wait for Farris in the FGH Building, but not for long. Being the impatient person that he was, he made a call to Lt. Lawson.

"Lawson, I want you to put out an A.P.B. on Farris G. Hamley." *All points bulletin* would have him arrested on site, wherever found. But Farris was gone. December 7th felt like just another wasted day for D.A. William Hawkins.

Down at the main desk of the university hospital in New York City, there was a moment of excitement.

"Dr. Berg, in my hand I have something I think you would want to see," Dr. Pantino said.

"What is it?" Dr. Berg asked.

"It is an anonymous donor kidney for Riff Marteen in room 112," Dr. Pantino said.

"Great! Let's run some tests on him and see if he's viable," Dr. Berg suggested.

Three hours had passed, and the results came back.

"Dr. Berg, you are not going to believe this..." Dr. Pantino said.

"What's that?" Dr. Berg asked.

"I ran a genetic profile on this anonymous donor, and it came back as a familial match," Dr. Pantino said.

"I guess if we get all of our paperwork signed, we can do the surgery tomorrow morning," Dr. Berg said with surprise for how fast things were coming together for their patient.

December 9th came very quickly. Riff got his new kidney, and the donor got a feeling of unconditional grace. He felt good all over!

After the operation, Dr. Pantino had a few words for Dr. Berg.

"I just can't believe it. The donor said that he was absolutely sure that he wasn't related," Dr. Pantino said.

"Well, so be it. It is what it is. Let's just take a win when it comes our way," Dr. Berg said.

"Oh, Dr. Berg, Riff wants to thank the donor. What should we do?" Dr. Pantino asked.

"We need to ask the donor while he is still here. Go ask him," Dr. Berg said.

Soon, the nurse wheeled the donor back into Riff's room.

"Say, don't I know you? You look familiar. I know that we have met before. Let me think! Yes, it was twenty years ago in Hawaii. You were the nervous kid that sold me that beach front land for twenty million dollars....what a steal that was! I made money on that deal," Riff said.

"Dr. Berg, I would like you to meet a friend of mine. This is Farris G. Hamley," Riff said.

"Riff, how do you feel?" Farris asked.

"Oh, I feel like twenty million bucks! Farris, I gotta ask you. Why did you do it? Why did you give me your kidney? It was like a miracle or something. Tell me why," Riff pressed for an answer.

"Well Riff, I just guess that I believe in happy endings," Farris said.

"You will get no argument from me. There must be something that I can do for you. I'd like to show you some gratitude. How about it?" Riff asked.

"Riff, there are two choices in life that you should look at," Farris said.

"What's that?" Riff asked.

"A person can be right about things, or he can be kind. If you ever must choose between one over the other, choose kindness. Nobody likes somebody that is always right. Nobody reasonable would ever say: 'I hate that person over there because he is just too kind to me,'" Farris said.

"I get it! I get what you are saying. Maybe it's time for me to mend my ways. Now that I think about it, I am tired of looking over my shoulder. Retirement is just a 'yes' away!" Riff said.

Dinner Time at the Hawkins House

December 8th, 2002

Well, things worked out handsomely for Riff by December 9th. Back in Los Angeles, things were not going so good for D.A. William Hawkins. His main suspect, Farris G. Hamley, had disappeared.

With nothing good happening, December 8th would just be another fruitless day. Maybe things would improve at dinner. Maybe!

There they were, William, Lora, and Lannie, about to sit down at the table together for supper when Lora made a crass remark.

"Well, it sure is nice that you could join us for dinner tonight, William. Lannie, it seems like we are honored with a special guest tonight. I wonder if he is going to stay for dessert," Lora said.

"Oh, come on Lora. There is no need to carry on like that. You know what my job is like. Please, can't we just enjoy supper?" William pleaded.

"So William, let's talk about your job. You must have locked up that awful Farris Hamley by now. You've been after him for the last three months. When can our home life get back to normal? Or is *this* the new normal?" Lora asked, looking dissatisfied.

"Mommy, why does daddy hate Farris Hamley?" Lannie asked.

"Lannie, daddy does not hate Farris Hamley. Daddy hates the bad things that he does," William said. His wife turned towards him.

"So, do you hate the fact that Farris is trying to build low-income housing for the poor?" Lora asked.

"Now, Lora, you know from what I've told you before. Things are not always simple. There are other things that I cannot talk about. So, let's drop it," William said.

For the rest of the dinner, the room was filled with silence. Lannie finished her food and was excused, so she went to her room. Then the real conversation began.

"William, for the last three months you have missed dinner with me and Lannie about three times a week. How long do you want to go on for? You know, some women would just pack up their bags and leave with the kid. Is that what you are encouraging me to do?" Lora wondered out loud.

"Now, Lora, don't talk that way. It is that way in the movies, but this is real life. We are all a family. It won't be this way forever. Things will get better," William insisted.

"Things will always get better? Are you sure? Somehow, I think in the back of my mind, with that job you have, there will always be another Farris Hamley to lock up. William, you need to step back and see what's really happening in the long run. Is your job worth the loss of your family life? Are you willing to trade our happiness for this career? For money? For some fancy award to hang on our wall? William, what is it that you really, really, really want? I would like to know," Lora said.

Just then the phone rang.

"We will talk later. I've gotta take this call," William said.

Lora had the phone receiver in her hand. She was in a slow burn of anger.

"Here, take the phone. It is your mistress calling," Lora said.

"Hello, this is William Hawkins speaking," William said.

"This is Captain Taylor. I just wanted to tell you that our morning meeting has been postponed until one o'clock. Something else has come up that needs my attention," Captain Taylor said.

"That's quite okay," William said as he hung up the phone.

"I suppose now we have got to give up some more of your time. Isn't that what your call was all about? It was about you, giving up your time for some righteous cause that demands too much from our family. William, you are gonna have to make some very important choices. You can give your job one hundred percent of your time and get a wall full of awards, or you can spend some quality time with your family. When is the last time that you talked with your daughter? Do you even know what she is doing in school? It would be nice if you would just stop and take a timeout for her. If you did, you would find out what an amazing daughter you have. Did you know about the project that she chose to do in school? All by herself, she chose to write Christmas cards for the senior citizens who are living in assisted living homes around the Los Angeles area," Lora said.

"She does that?" William asked with surprise.

William looked down, as if he felt ashamed. He knew Lora was talking straight. William had hardly ever talked to Lannie about her schoolwork or anything going on in her life.

"William, I once heard that honest, faithful men would always keep their priorities straight – God, family, and country. William, please don't mess with that order. Don't put family last! We love you. Lannie is just a little girl and yet she sees that people are more important than things. I hope that you can appreciate her joy," Lora said.

"I do! I very much do! I'll try to do better. No, I *will* do better. Lora, I love you both," William said.

"Thank you, William, you know love is also an action that people learn from those who teach through their example. Lannie is spot on," Lora said.

Just then the phone rang again.

"I can't believe it. There it is again. When will this nightmare be over? You know William, that phone has rang maybe twenty times this week alone. Who could it be this time?" Lora asked while picking up the phone.

"It's for you," Lora said to William.

"Hello, this is Lt. Lawson. Captain Taylor wants to know if you got any phone calls today from New York about Hamley," Lt. Lawson asked.

"Tell him I'll give him a full update tomorrow morning," William said as he hung up.

"William, you have spent too much of your time – no, our time – on this Farris Hamley case. What if, after all of this time, you find out that he is innocent of all those crimes?" Lora asked.

"Not a chance!" William replied with confidence.

"But, what if!" Lora said.

"If that happens, then I will quit from the Los Angeles District Attorney's office and find a nine to five job," William said.

The following week was December 14th. This morning there was a meeting in the D.A.'s office. The purpose was the usual, unofficial daily update on the Hamley case.

At this meeting was the typical crew: Captain Taylor, Lt. Lawson, D.A. Hawkins. Today, they had a special guest, Commissioner Vance Randle. Captain Taylor began this meeting with a few words of encouragement.

"Gentlemen, what did the city boy die of when he was lost in the woods?" Silence filled the room. "Well, the city boy died of shame because he never prepared for the unexpected. That is not going to happen to us. When we go into court, we will have all of our ducks in a row. The evidence keeps piling up. Farris Hamley does not know who he is dealing with," Captain Taylor said.

As luck would have it, on that very same day, Farris G. Hamley was seen entering the FGH Building. Lt. Lawson made the arrest and immediately called up Hawkins.

"D.A. Hawkins, we've got him!" Lt. Lawson said.

Hawkins broke out into a great big smile.

Farris Arrested,
Grand Jury Fiasco

December 14th, 2002

Farris Hamley was waiting in his holding cell for the next grand jury meeting, which was going to be held the following day.

At ten that morning, Farris was in the grand jury room and D.A. Hawkins began his indictment.

"Members of the grand jury, I intend to show that Farris G. Hamley did order up the attempted murder of Jason Zauler, a known employee and whistleblower for FGH Corporation. How do I know this? What I have right here in my hand is a memo note, written on a corporate memo pad, taken from the office of Farris Hamley. Clearly, this is Hamley's letterhead on the note and on the bottom of this note, is his signature. Furthermore, once I confronted him about this Grand Jury indictment proceedings, Farris Hamley fled the state for parts unknown. Clearly, he was in fear of a subpoena or arrest. That was, without a doubt, an obstruction of justice. His intentions were quite clear. I intend to show that this is typical, normal behavior for Farris G. Hamley. I have in this courtroom a person of interest that will give sworn testimony as to his character. I give you a Mr. Clayton Burrows. Mr. Burrows, will you please take the stand and state your full name and take your oath," D.A. Hawkins said.

"My name is Clayton Burrows. I am the lead accountant for FGH Corporation," Clayton said.

"And how did you get that job?" D.A. Hawkins asked. Clay was silent.

"Did you ever work for Club Lotus in Kansas City?" Hawkins asked. Again, silence.

"Mr. Burrows, do you know the penalty for withholding evidence from a grand jury?" D.A. Hawkins asked. Again, silence.

"Okay, Mr. Burrows. Let's talk about something more current. Let's talk about the Girrard Company. Did you and your boss, Farris Hamley, purchase substandard building materials for a low-income housing project on the south side of Los Angeles?" Hawkins asked.

Suddenly there was an outburst from the crowd seated in the courtroom. It came from Willie Reed, Farris' lifetime friend from Sailors Hill.

"Stop! Stop it right now. Your honor, I have got to stop these proceedings. Farris Hamley has done nothing wrong. D.A. Hawkins needs to recuse himself from these proceedings. He has a prejudicial interest in this case," Willie said.

"And how might that be?" Hawkins asked.

"You, you...you don't even know who you really are," Willie said.

"What do you mean by that?" D.A. Hawkins asked.

"You know, William, you really are not plugged into this entire thing, are you? There are a lot of things that you really don't know anything about. For instance, the very man that you are trying to lock up, because he seems to be, in your eyes, a criminal is anything but a criminal. For years, he has given away almost two billion dollars to needy causes. Yesterday, at two o'clock he signed over the FGH Building to the City of Los Angeles to be used as a government center. And then, there is that other thing..." Willie said.

"If you would allow me a few minutes I will tell you an interesting story. It's a story that needs to be told. Long ago, in the city of San Francisco, there was a man and his wife on vacation. When they were on vacation, the wife got pregnant. Before telling her husband, she ran away to parts unknown. Years went by, this woman raised her son with another man. He grew up to become a district attorney. That D.A. is you. You are the son of Farris G. Hamley...and your mother is Annie," Willie Reed declared.

Suddenly, the judge slammed his gavel down.

"That's it! I want everybody associated with this case to go to my personal chambers," the judge said.

Once inside the judge's chambers, the judge asked Willie Reed for real proof that Farris was indeed D.A. Hawkins' father.

"Proof! So, you want proof. Let's ask Hawkins' mother. She is standing in the hallway outside of the courtroom," Willie said.

Annie was soon escorted into the judges' chambers. William had a surprised look on his face. In fact, at this point, he was speechless. It was like all the oxygen had left the room.

As Annie entered the chambers, she walked over to Farris and hugged him.

"William, how do you think that you got the middle name 'Grant.' That is Farris's middle name," Annie said.

At this point in time an assistant to the judge came over and whispered something into his ear.

"Sir, this Hamley has a reputation as being some sort of socialist Santa Claus. You know judge, it might not look good in the newspaper if you locked up Santa Claus just before Christmas. And think of the elections coming up. This might all blow up in your face," the assistant whispered.

"It is my ruling that I will take this entire case under advisement for a later date," the judge said.

The chambers were cleared and outside of the courtroom people crowded around and began talking. D.A. Hawkins just departed with his head hanging low, when Lt. Lawson approached him with some new evidence.

"Sir, sir, Mr. Hawkins, sir. You are not going to believe this. This is a basket taken from the office waste of Clayton Burrows. The janitor in the building still had his waste stored in the basement at FGH. Just look at some of those papers. It looks like Clayton Burrows was practicing the signature of Farris Hamley. My guess is that he was the one who wrote that memo note. Maybe he was behind the attempted hit on Jason Zauler. Not Farris!" Lt. Lawson said.

"Yeah, it looks that way," D.A. Hawkins said.

"There is something else. I did some checking into that Clayton Burrows character. It's not his real name. It is Claud Bennet. He is wanted in Puerto Rico for forgery, and he is a person of interest in a missing person's case. It seems that he forged somebody's name on a land deal. Afterwards, that forgery victim of his disappeared. Bennet sold his property. The whole transaction was a fraud. There is a warrant out for his arrest," Lt. Lawson said.

"Sure, the whole thing makes sense. I messed up big time, Lt. Lawson. I gotta ask you. What is the biggest enemy of wisdom?" Hawkins said.

The lieutenant shook his head as if saying he didn't know. Then Lawson guessed ignorance.

"No!" D.A. Hawkins responded.

"The biggest enemy of wisdom is illusionary wisdom. That is when you are certain about something and then you find out that you were completely wrong," Hawkins said with humility in his voice.

Once the crowd dispersed from the hallway outside, Hawkins noticed that Farris and his mother were walking off together arm in arm. He felt ashamed!

D.A. Hawkins got a few steps away from Lt. Lawson when, Lawson said with a clear voice, "I also did some checking with the FBI and all that money that Farris accumulated was clean. He's good to go," Lt. Lawson said.

As D.A. William Hawkins arrived at home, there was a shadow of shame following him.

As he stood in front of his door at home, he could barely turn the handle. What was he going to say to his wife and daughter? After all that boasting at the dinner table, what would be his new words of wisdom about locking away that giant mobster, Farris Hamley? Hawkins dreaded the reality of his folly.

Once dinnertime was well underway, William answered Lora's big questions.

"How did your day go for you? Is there anything of joy that you would like to share with us?" Lora asked, waiting for the expected story of criminal defeat.

William told the whole story about the day's fiasco. Lora became an earnest listener. She never once said 'I told you so!' and fully embodied graciousness. This quality of hers made William's heart swell with so much love for her.

Mountain Cabin, Christmas Eve

December 24th, 2002

After the revelations that arose in court, William G. Hawkins felt very mortified. He was slow to heal, but being that Christmas was soon approaching, he didn't want to spoil the mood, so he put on a smile, however inauthentic.

Lora wished for a snowy Christmas, so she had made reservations to spend the Christmas holiday at a large cabin up in the foothills of the Sierra Madre Mountains on Christmas Eve. Her guest list was quite eclectic: her husband, her daughter, and three surprise guests.

William, Lora, and Lannie got to the cabin first. The main meal was planned to be served at five o'clock.

As William was bringing the suitcases in from the car to the house, he turned to his daughter Lannie for a few pleasant words.

"Lannie, if you have a little patience, you might be lucky enough to see a mountain bluebird. The Native Americans around here believe that if you do, you will experience some godly joy, so be very watchful," William said with a wink.

Once they were all unpacked, Lora came over to Lannie and handed her an envelope.

"Here, Lannie, this letter came in the mail yesterday," Lora said. Lannie opened up the envelope and read the Christmas card out loud.

> *Lannie, I got your Christmas card a couple of days ago. It really cheered me up. You must be a very special joy for your parents, to have such a loving and caring daughter as you. Lannie it is not easy being alone at Christmas, especially when I have outlived all my friends and siblings. Your joy has warmed my heart.*
>
> *Love,*
> *Bo Lukka*

Everybody smiled. Soon, Lora started to prepare hors d'oeuvres for the company that was coming. Outside it was starting to snow and Lannie stood patiently looking out the window for that mountain bluebird. All she could see was snow, slowly drifting down.

William was sitting in a chair and looking at his daughter by the window. From his point of view, all he could see was the back of Lannie's head, which had two neatly braided curls laying down over her shoulders.

Soon there was a knock on the cabin door. Lora went to answer the door. The guests were two familiar faces. It was Farris and Willie. Lora took their coats and walked them into the living room. The look on William's face was very uneasy, but he offered them both a hot brandy. They accepted and were seated.

The smell of turkey and the silence of everyone filled the room. Over by the cabin door was a Christmas present in a good–sized box with small holes across the top. It was wrapped in Christmas paper and the name tag read, 'Merry Christmas, Lannie'. The box started to move. Farris spoke up.

"That's for Lannie, I guess we can't wait any longer," Farris said.

Lannie ran over to the door and brought the box back to the tree.

"Let her open it," Farris said.

Lannie opened the box and let out a great big smile, saying, "Ohhhh, it's what I always wanted. It's a tabby kitten."

"His name is Scooter, he's a very loyal friend," Farris said.

Lannie held the kitten and walked over to the cabin window holding and petting her new best friend, Scooter.

Once again, there was a knock at the door. Lora went over and opened it. There, with the snow gently falling on her face, stood Annie, Farris's estranged wife and mother to William. Being that it was Christmas Eve, everybody wore a friendly, cordial face.

This cordial situation was about to become a test for everybody's heart. The room's silence was interrupted by a child's voice. It was Lannie.

"Oh look, look outside the window, there is a mountain bluebird on a branch in front of our window. Oh, the joy of it all!" Lannie said.

Suddenly, all of the Christmas guests got up out of their seats and walked over to the window. In an instant, all of the adults raised their glasses for a Christmas toast. This toast had a profound effect on everybody's mood. They soon became friendly.

Farris and William stepped off to the side and then William began a conversation with Farris. Annie went to sit down in a chair.

"Farris, do you think that I am an honest man?" William asked.

"Yes, I think I do!" Farris answered.

"Well, what's the worst thing that an honest man can do?" William asked.

Farris just shook his head and shrugged his shoulders.

"The worst thing that an honest man can do is… to make an honest mistake. Farris, let there be peace between us and let it begin with me," William said as he extended his hand in friendship.

Without waiting for a second, Farris filled William's hand with a firm handshake and smile.

"All is forgiven, son," Farris spoke loudly and clearly.

Farris and William stood there in the middle of the room and hugged each other. This moment was not to be wasted. Annie got up out of her seat and made it a group hug. For all three of them, they made it their best Christmas ever.

Lannie turned around and witnessed their hug. She sensed that there was a great peace of mind. Moments later, Lannie turned back and looked out the window. Suddenly, some clouds parted, and a sunbeam came down from above. It shined on the bluebird and on Lannie's face. With her gentle small voice she said, "Merry Christmas to one and all."

The End

Epilogue

Before the end of Christmas Eve dinner, there was another unexpected guest. Lora went over and opened the door upon hearing another knock. It was a man with a paper rolled up in his hand.

"Excuse me, ma'am. I was wondering if there is a Farris Hamley here?" he said.

"Why yes, I'll get him for you. Why don't you come in out of the snow," Lora insisted?

"Oh no, I don't want to spoil his Christmas. Here, could you give him this paper? And could you tell him that it is from Riff? Now that I'm retired, I wanted him to have it. Tell him I said Merry Christmas. Would you please do that?" Riff turned and walked away before getting an answer.

Lora gave the paper to Farris. Farris opened it up and saw that it was a construction contract paid-in-full for a swimming pool in the shape of a kidney!

Van Muessen

by
Jerry McCallson

Foreword

In the vast void, there appeared a significant light. This light was like no other, for it possessed an emerald ray. In the center of this emerald ray was a round white core with a golden mass. This golden mass surrounded the center core.

In an instant, the light had a voice. The voice summoned a smaller light to appear before him.

"Raphael, Raphael, present yourself. There are words that need to be spoken. As you know, the bright morning star has deceived one third of your former peers. All confusion will soon pass.

Your brother, Michael, will soon execute his assignment. Before such, I will redeem the repentant lost. For sure, I have said in the past, that the Earth is not a playground. Be sure to know, that the harvest will surely be.

Raphael, there is one soul that shows great promise, I want you to engage the one called by the name of Louris Van Muessen. And so, his story began. Yahweh spoke.

A Place Where Souls Are Sent To Be Harvested

Introduction to
Van Muessen

Earth... the place where souls are sent to be harvested.

It was the spring of 1998. In the world of politics, the war in Northern Ireland was finally winding down. The Good Friday Peace Agreement set in motion a changing of attitudes in Ireland. Was that so back on Summit Hill, in St. Paul Minnesota?

Sometimes, old ways die hard. Maybe, just maybe, there might be a good moral harvest at 2010 Pearl Street. Sometimes it takes a real-life crisis to define a person's character. Could that somebody be Derry O'Konner?

Derry's wife, Allison, believes that all bad behavior is pure junk. Just how much junk could she put up with from her husband, Derry?

Derry O'Konner is a retired successful industrialist who made millions by wheeling and dealing and controlling people on the outside business world. Now he is faced with the struggle of personal relationships inside his own family. Namely, his daughter Amy.

For a man that was used to getting his own way, could he find compromise within his home, or would he insist on control? Surely, he couldn't expect to manage his daughter's love life. Just who was this outsider who was stealing her heart?

For Derry, it didn't matter. He believed that he could handle any situation, but was he ready for a man called Louris Van Muessen?

Van Muessen

1959 (age 9)

Faas and Else Van Muessen (Louris's parents) just came back from a teacher's conference.

"What's going on with Louris?" Else asked Faas.

"I don't know, but I am going to find out" Faas answered. The serious look on Faas's face seemed to summarize the whole conference experience.

"Louris, could you come out into the kitchen? I would like to have a word with you." Fass called out to Louris.

"Louris, your teacher has told us that you give a boy named Arnie money every day before lunch at school. I want to know right now if that is true and how long has this been going on?" Faas demanded.

"I am sorry, but I can't say." Louris said.

"Very well, go to your room and every day from now on, after school, stay in your room until supper. Is that understood?" Faas said.

"Oh, now Faas, don't be so hard on the boy. I am sure there is a good reason." Else said to Faas.

Good reason, I am sure there is. I'll just bet you that he is paying some school bully money to keep from being beaten up. I will not stand for my son becoming a coward. He can just sit in his room and have some quality time thinking about his actions." Faas spoke in anger.

"Oh, Faas, you have got to bend once in a while. Sometimes life is not as clear as the beautiful blue sky.

Let go of some of that anger and maybe things will all work out for the best." Else said to Faas.

"Oh, you always say things like that" Faas responded.

"Listen Else, my father Ader raised me with too much kindness, and it got him nowhere. Everybody said that he was a softie, a pushover. Well, not me! My son is going to be a man among men. A leader in the community. A man that everybody looks up to. That starts with being firm. Yes, firmness is the way to go" Faas lectured Else.

At suppertime everybody was quiet. The silence at the table was interrupted by an occasional; Pass-the-salt please. For two weeks, each day Louris would finish his supper and go directly to his room. Finally, one day Faas had some free time, so he went back to his son's school. He wanted to talk again to Louris's teacher, Mrs. Adams.

"Mrs. Adams, could you please give me an update on Louris." Faas asked.

"Yes, Mr. Van Muessen, your son still gives Arnie Peterson money each day, but now I have noticed something different" Mrs. Adams said.

"What's that?" Faas asked Mrs. Adams.

"Well, Louris took the coat that he was wearing, right off his back and gave it to Arnie Peterson."

"What?" Fass shouted in a rage.

"You need to do something about that boy!" Mrs. Adams said.

As expected, Faas went back home in his rage. Standing in the kitchen, with fierce demand, he shouted.

"Louris, come out of your room. I want to talk to you in the kitchen. Now!" Faas demanded.

"What is it? Louris asked.

"Louris, where is that jacket grandma Mina gave you a few years ago for Christmas? Where is it?" Faas yelled out. Louris looked down at the floor.

"I gave it to Arnie Peterson."

"You did what?" Faas asked.

"I gave it to Arnie because he was always cold." Louris said.

"And the money, what about the money? Why are you giving away your school lunch money? Why? What is with that? Is Arnie Peterson shaking you down? Answer me right now!" Faas demanded.

Louris sat there in silence for a few moments. Just then, Faas raised his right hand up as if he were going to slap Louris in the face, when Else came into the kitchen. Louris just looked up at Faas with his eyes wide open.

"But dad, I gave him money because he is very poor, and he never gets to eat 3 full meals in a day. I eat until I am completely full 3 times each day. My breakfast is very large and the same is for all of my suppers. He never does. His dad is too proud to take money away from the school lunch program. So, he has to go without lunch. I gave him the money because he is my friend. I gave him my jacket because the sleeves were too short for me, and Arnie was always cold. So, I gave it to him." Louris said.

At this point, Faas dropped his hand down to his side. Faas moved his face to the right and then dropped his head towards the floor.

"Dad, I just wanted to be like you." Louris said with tears in his eyes. Silence then filled the room.

Faas moved over to where Louris was sitting and put his hand on Louris's shoulder. Louris rose up from his chair and in an instant they stood, hugging each other. A smile came across Else's Face.

"Faas, you have done something very good. You have raised our son to be kind. Arnie was hungry, Louris fed him. Arnie was cold, so Louris clothed him. Didn't our own pastor say as much during one of his Sunday sermons? His words fell on Louris's ears. Remember what the pastor said."

"Pray, believe, do." Else said. From that day on, Else made sure that there would always be peace in the house at 1910 Bergen Street, Lanesboro Minnesota.

The Lucky Coin

Age 12
The House of 1910 Bergen Street

"Ader Van Muessen, the grandfather of Louris, had been walking in a fast pace all around the house for the last 15 minutes. Ader, what's the problem?" Else demanded.

"Oh, I knew it was Louris's 12th birthday and I forgot his birthday present back at the apartment. What should I do?" asked Ader.

"Well, I have heard you jingle all of those coins in your pocket. Why don't you just give him a few coins? That will be just fine" Else said.

"You think so?" Ader replied.

"I know so!" Else said.

"Oh Louris, could you come here for a minute?" Ader said as Else left the room. She went back into the kitchen. Louris came into the living room. It was just Ader and Louris, face to face. Ader reached into his pocket and pulled out an old silver dollar. Ader looked down into Louris's eyes.

"You see the nick on the edge of this silver dollar? I put that nick there when I was about your age. I made that nick just to see if this coin would find its way back to me after I spent it. Somehow it always found its way back into my pocket. It always came back just when I needed it the most. Here, it is now yours. Happy Birthday Louris." Ader handed Louris the coin.

Louris retreated to his bedroom and placed the coin on top of his dresser. At nighttime, he laid on his bed and stared at his bedroom ceiling. He tried to imagine what magic or good luck would come from owning such a coin.

Soon morning came. As Louris was on his back, the silence of his bedroom was interrupted by a sudden thump. It was his coin. It was in the middle of the floor spinning in a fast circle. Soon the coin came to a sudden stop and flattened out onto the floor. Louris picked up the coin and started to talk to it.

"You have value, I can see you have greater worth than just one dollar. From now on we are friends for life. You are my lucky coin." Louris said.

These years 9–12 were very fruitful years. For Louris had received his basic faith training from his pastor and both his parents Faas and Else. It was time to put all of that faith training into practice. In the following years, he did exactly that. From that point on, he moved closer and closer to finding out the what and why of his being. He became a kind and virtuous person with an optimistic attitude even in the face of temptation and adversity.

Twelve years had passed by since Louris had received his lucky coin from grandfather Ader. Louris could not make a living on his only passion, painting. Though he was talented he struggled to get by. He needed full-time job. So, he worked at a canning company as a production worker. Whenever possible, he began teaching local students who shared his enthusiasm for art. Little did he know, something significant was about to change his mundane life.

Raphael Calls Harlan

"Harlan, Harlan, what are you doing?" Raphael, a voice in the sky asked.

"Who is it?" Harlan asked.

"It is me, Raphael."

"Oh, I am just walking through the rolling hills overlooking the town of Lanesboro" Harlan responded.

"Harlan, there is a town overlook a short distance in front of you to the west. Go there now. There is a bench next to a mulberry tree in full bloom. It has ripe fruit on its branches. Meet me there in about 30 minutes." Raphael said.

Harlan nodded his head as he continued his walk. Thirty minutes passed and Raphael patiently waited for Harlan to arrive.

"Where is he?" Raphael said, as he looked over his right shoulder. Along came Harlan; he was a medium build but tall figured man. Dressed in hiking clothes and walking with the aid of a walking stick. His hands were rough and worn. They were wrapped in cuts, scrapes, and calluses but he was proud of them. His right hand was branded by 3 brown moles that were very pronounced. Harlan approached Raphael with a smirk.

"Harlan, are you going to make it? If you walked any slower, people might think you were a Greek statue. I've been waiting here for almost forty minutes." Raphael said with a half grin.

"You know Raphael, I think I might be slow because of a thorn in my toe." Harlan said.

"Let me see. Place your foot up on my lap and I'll take a look at it." Raphael said.

"Sure thing, happy to do it" Harlan responded.

"Okay, it seems like you do have a hitchhiker. If it were any larger, you would have enough wood to build a house. Here, let me remove it for you" Raphael said.

"Ouch! That's not the thorn. You are pulling my toe off!" Harlan yelled.

"That's right! It's a mistake and that's why you are here. To help correct something." Raphael said. Harlan sat there in silence and looked out over the town of Lanesboro with Raphael at his side.

"Have you ever seen such a blue sky? Just look at that sky. It's so clear; a person could see forever." Harlan said.

"Harlan, that is why I have chosen you to be a helping hand. You have clarity. Clarity is a gift. Not many have it. You appreciate it. It is always good to work with you." Raphael said.

"Thanks for the confidence" Harlan said.

"Now, Harlan be still. I will place into your mind what I want you to do. It won't take very long, just focus." Raphael said.

Harlan sat in complete silence. Without words Harlan nodded at his friend and got up. He exhaled, paused, and then proceeded to walk down the hill towards Lanesboro.

Harlan Morphed into a Man

Something happened to Harlan's appearance. He had morphed into a businessman dressed in a suit; briefcase included. By all standard assumptions, he looked like a door-to-door salesman. Yet, there he was, just another stranger coming to town. For a brief moment, he stood in front of a road sign. It said, "Welcome to Lanesboro, the Center of Bluff Country."

Harlan continued his walk and past the sign on the road, until he reached a house at the beginning of town. It was the house at 1015 Moro Street. This was Lilah's Bed and Breakfast. There was a "no vacancy" sign on the front porch. Harlan walked up the stairs and rang the doorbell. Out came an elderly lady with a smile on her face.

"Hello, my name is Harlan" Harlan stated.

"I know, we have been expecting you for about 2 hours. My name is Lilah Mundson. My goodness, I saw you walking down the street towards our B&B. Say, have you got a lame foot or something? If you walked any slower, you could lose a race with a glacier." Lilah said with a smirk. Harlan looked puzzled for about 5 seconds and then smiled.

"I see, you've been talking with Raphael, haven't you?" Harlan said with a smile.

"Maybe" Lilah said.

"Okay bring me up to speed. Where do you want me to stay? Harlan asked.

"Your room is ready. Just follow me." Lilah said. They went down the hallway together. Lilah stopped at room 104. "This is where you will be staying. All of the necessary information about my bed and breakfast is listed on a card on the dresser next to your bed. We will see you at supper. Supper is at 6:00 P.M. sharp in the dining room off to the left." Lilah said.

"Well Lilah, since you have been talking to Raphael, I guess you know why I am here" Harlan said.

"Yes, it's about a young man that lives at 1910 Bergen Street. The lad's name is Louris Van Muessen. Raphael seems to think that he needs a little nudge in the right direction." Lilah explained.

"You have spoken well" Harlan said.

"Oh Harlan, we will be having supper with 2 other guests: Walley Sherman and Archie Morgan. See you at supper" Lilah said as she walked away.

At 6:00 P.M. everyone was seated in the dining room. Lilah, Harlan, Walley and Archie.

"Harlan, this is Archie Morgan and Walley Sherman. Archie, Walley, this is Harlan Wartzwinkle" Lilah said.

"Well, Mr. Morgan and Mr. Sherman, what line of work are you both in?" Harlan asked.

"Please, everyone here uses first names" Lilah said.

"I work down at Walley's garage, I am the owner. Archie works, well, I'll let him answer that." Walley said.

"What line of work are you in?" Walley asked Harlan.

"I am here in town to answer an ad in the newspaper. It seems that the bank is looking for a Finance Officer. I am scheduled for an interview tomorrow morning." Harlan said.

"I am sure everything will go well for you at that time" Walley said.

"Yes, I am sure you will get the job" Archie said with assurance. Everyone at the table did their small talk and then left for their daily jobs.

The following evening, Lilah stopped Harlan in the hallway and asked him if he had gotten the job.

"Most certainly" replied Harlan.

"Good, then I take it that everything is on schedule" Lilah said.

"It is" replied Harlan as he entered his room for the evening.

The next day, Percy Penrod (the bank president) came into Harlan's office as Harlan was seated at his desk.

"Harlan, I know that this is a little out of the ordinary, but I need you to do a special job for me. After reading your resume, I was very impressed by all of your qualifications. I made some phone calls to your previous employer. It seems that you are qualified to do all the positions in the banking system. So, with that said, I want you to go over to 1910 Bergen Street and give Mr. Faas Van Meussen his final eviction notice. I want you to be firm about it. Time is money". Percy said.

"I'll do my best Mr. Penrod." Harlan said.

Eviction Notice Served

At 4:00 P.M., there he was. Yes, it was Harlan Wartzwinkle sitting in his car in front of 1910 Bergen Street – a place where Harlan did not want to be.

"Time is money. Be firm. What Percy really meant was, to be indifferent and cruel". Harlan said what he thought about the situation. His main thought was: why me? It goes against my purpose driven creed. I need to just calm myself down and mellow out. "I know, I'll turn on the radio and defuse."

The song that was playing was "Why me Lord?"

"Great! That's all I need is more guilt." He then turned and looked straight ahead. From his peripheral vision, he noticed a figure of a person next to him. This was no person, it was Raphael.

"You don't want to be unkind, do you?" Raphael said.

"No! It goes against my very being" Harlan said.

"Harlan, how many times have you heard the saying there is a reason for the season?"

"I know, but still." Harlan responded.

"Okay Harlan, you need to know a little more information. So here goes. Harlan, there are so many lukewarm souls out there and fake posturing has become the norm. It is my understanding that the good Lord wants to know if Louris Van Muessen is the real deal. Is he part of the elect? He could be chosen for a great blessing. I am sure you have heard.

"In fire, gold is tested and worthy men in the crucible of humiliation. Harlan you are playing a major part of Louris's discovery blessing." Raphael said.

"I guess we are all tested sooner or later" Harlan said to an empty car seat. For Raphael was now gone.

After pause Harlan left his car and started to pound on the Van Muessen door. Soon the door opened.

"Is this the Van Muessen residence? I would like to speak to Mr. Faas Van Muessen. Is he available?" Harlan asked. A soft voice answered through a crack in the door.

"Faas is not at home right now. He has to work late. He will be home later in the evening." Else said.

"Are you Mrs. Van Muessen?" Harlan asked.

"Yes, I am Else Van Muessen, his wife." Else replied.

"I am Harlan Wartzwinkle from your bank" Harlan said.

At this time Louris came out from his bedroom and stood behind his mother Else. Harlan's right hand extended through the crack in the door. In his hand was the eviction notice.

"It is the last one that you will get. You have missed your last mortgage payment. Our bank is sick and tired of this routine. You people are always a day late and a dollar short. The next time you hear a knock on your door, it will be the sheriff. You only have until Friday to make good on your mortgage. If not, you will be escorted off the premises."

Harlan extended his right hand through the doorway and handed Else the notice.

Before Harlan withdrew his hand, Louris noticed that he had 3 brown moles near his thumb. Harland withdrew his hand after Else grabbed the notice. Else then closed the door and stood in the center of the living room with the eviction notice pressed against her heart. Slowly she stared at the floor in painful silence.

Louris rushed towards the door and yelled out to Harlan.

"You are an evil, evil man!"

Harlan got back into his car, clenched his fists while gripping the steering wheel, and drove off.

"Wow! Now that was the worst thing I have ever said to a human being." Harlan said as he drove away.

Back in the living room at 1910 Bergen Street, Else stood in the middle of the floor. Still pressing the eviction notice against her heart. Florence Henders, who was sitting on the living room couch had witnessed the whole incident. She had only just arrived and Else had not told her of their recent struggles, of Fass's injury, or of the difficulties finding work after the incident. Florence uncomfortably looked at the floor in disbelief.

She was Else's best friend, but they didn't know what to say to each other. The whole embarrassment was too much for everyone.

"I think I need to go now." Florence said as she quietly closed the door behind her.

The entire living room was silent, but not for long. Louris began his rant.

"Harlan was a mean, mean man. I hate him. I hope something very bad happens to him." Louris said in anger.

Quickly, Else walked over to Louris and looked straight into his eyes and spoke.

"No Louris, I won't hear of such talk. Remember what our pastor Jorgensen said during last Sunday's sermon? He said:

"We all need to hate the sin and not the sinner. We need to separate the sin from the person. He reminded us of that bible scripture Romans 11:32 (God has confounded us all, so that he can give mercy to us all.) Now isn't that fair?" Else said.

"I guess so. Oh, you always say things like that." Louris said.

"Louris, I know that Harlan Wartzwinkle spoke very rough and unkind, but don't let that be an excuse for you to harden your heart. Don't become the monster that you hate. Instead, become the good person that you always wanted to have as a friend. If you do that, you will see days that are greater than tomorrow." Else said.

"But mom, that is all fine and dandy, but what are we going to do about the mortgage money? Where is that going to come from?" Louris said.

"Pray, believe, do." Else said.

"How is that going to pay the bills?" Louris asked.

"That is something we need to talk over with your father Faas." Else said.

At suppertime the three of them were seated at the table; it was Faas, Louris and Else. Else hesitantly mentioned their visitor and the mortgage payment that was due Friday.

"You know that brown jacket of mine in the closet, the brown one that has zipper pockets? Well, inside the right pocket is enough money to pay that mortgage. I just knew that someday we would be hurting for cash, so I saved some. Don't worry your hearts about a thing." Faas said with a smile.

"You know, Faas and Louris, I think that we need to say grace before we eat." Else said.

"You go ahead and send up some good words, Else." Faas said.

"Good lord, thanks for not making us rich or poor and continue to make us better Christians. Amen." Else said.

After supper, Louris retreated to his room. He flopped on his bed silently studying the cracks in the ceiling. This was quite common for Louris. Over the years, he acquired the knowledge of where every imperfection, discoloration, chipped paint, and crack lived.

Thoughts, angry thoughts, centered on that visit from Harlan. This was a man that Louris never ever got to look at face-to-face. All Louris ever saw was that mole specked hand, sticking through a partially opened door that held the family eviction notice. Even when Harlan left for his car, all Louris saw was his back. When Friday came, Faas had to go to work. It was Louris's job to get the money out of Faas's jacket and go to the bank and make the late mortgage payment. Little did he realize that there was a late fee attached to the late payment.

Once at the bank, Louris went straight into Harlan's private office.

"Here is our mortgage payment" Louris said.

"That is all fine, but you still need to come up with the late fee. Then you are okay" Harlan said.

On hearing this, Louris went over to the teller and withdrew all of his personal savings for the late fee.

"Once again, you are still a day late and a dollar short" Harlan said.

"You heard me! You are a dollar short." Harlan said.

Louris could barely restrain himself, when suddenly he got an idea. That lucky silver dollar. He remembered the lucky dollar that Grandfather Ader had given him. The one with the nick on it.

Louris wasted no time. He went back to 1910 Bergen Street, his home, and got the answered prayer, his lucky silver dollar.

Louris soon arrived back at the bank. When he entered Harlan's office, all of the mortgage papers were on his desk. Harlan took the silver dollar and put his back to Louris. In a soft voice and a great big smile on his face, he whispered to himself.

"Job well done Louris. I was praying for you."

That evening, back at Lilah's B & B, Harlan was stopped by Lilah in the hallway. She waved him over to the kitchen for a little chat.

"Say Harlan, how did things go with Louris today?" Lilah asked.

"Oh, I followed my instructions from Raphael. I was told to be very aggressive with the eviction notice and Louris rose to the occasion. Faas and Else have truly raised a selfless young man. I think my work here is done, at least for the time being." Harland said.

The next morning there was an empty seat at the breakfast table. It was Harlan's. Lilah was busy going back and forth to the kitchen. Each time she was bringing additional food to the breakfast table. She stopped at the sink and looked through the kitchen screen. What she saw was Harlan. He was walking down a narrow road, singing along his way. The song he was singing was, well, "Why me Lord". In the distance was the sun's rays breaking through the clouds. Those sun rays were guiding him to the foothills of Lanesboro.

As Lilah turned her face towards the kitchen table to pick up a potholder, in an instant, she looked back towards Harlan. He was gone.

That evening back at 1910 Bergen Street, Faas called Louris into the kitchen.

"Louris, could you please come into the kitchen? I would like to have a word with you. Your mother has gone over to her sister's place in Harmony. She left a note on the table. She explained everything that happened today at the bank.

"Son, I am so very proud to call you my son. You have put grace before materialism. I have a great feeling that the good Lord has a great plan for you." Faas spoke with tears in his eyes.

Five days later, Else sent Louris to the store to get a loaf of bread. She sent him with a 5-dollar bill. Louris bought the bread and received some change. In the change was a silver dollar. The same one that grandfather Ader gave him. The nicked coin has found its way back into the hands of Louris. For a few seconds Louris just looked at his lucky coin and smiled.

"For some unknown reason, I need to keep this silver dollar" Louris said.

Two years had passed by since Louris had met Harlan at the bank. Harlan was still walking through the hills of Lanesboro just enjoying the beauty of life.

On top of a hill, in a quaint meadow, a voice called out. It was a familiar voice.

"Harlan, Harlan, what are you doing?"

Harlan stopped for a few seconds and said to himself, "I think I need to change my name to Pete." Harlan said with a smile.

"Harlan, Harlan," Raphael called out.

"You know Raphael, I bet you want me to go back into Lanesboro. Why is it every time you have me go back into that town, I feel like I need to wear a bulletproof vest?" Harlan said with a smile.

"Harlan, I see you haven't lost your sense of humor. It is good that you can still laugh. Laughter is the language of the creator" Raphael said.

"Okay, what is it?" Harlan asked.

"We need to talk over by our mulberry tree." Raphael said.

"Mulberry tree? What is it with you and those mulberry trees?" Harlan asked.

"I can't really say, but just be there" Raphael said.

"Here we go again. My mind is ready. Let's have it" Harlan requested.

Raphael gave his instructions without a word spoken.

Harlan Becomes Harmen

"So, as I understand the thoughts that you place in my mind, you are saying you want me to change my name and being to a new person. That person is Harmenzoon Van Rijn. You want me to become him." Harlan said.

"Yes, and I want you to go into the town of Lanesboro for a short time." Raphael said. Meanwhile, back at the house at 1910 Bergen Street, Louris and his mother Else were having a discussion.

"Louris's grandfather Ader is going to be 86 years old on Saturday. We are planning to give him a cake. In the meantime, why don't you go and visit with him for a while? He would love to have some company." Else said.

The affectionate rays of the Minnesota sun painted the maple and oak trees as they danced in the breeze. Louris took a short walk over to grandfather Ader's nursing home. After greeting, they both engaged in small talk about the beautiful weather. Suddenly Louris was drawn over to the wall at the foot of Ader's bed.

"Wow! What a life-like portrait of a beautiful lady. I can't get over it. It looks like a real person" Louris said.

"It is a real person. It is your grandmother, Mina Lynn when she was 19 years old in 1938. That is when I painted her." Ader said with a proud smile.

"How did you ever learn to paint so well? Masterful, just masterful." Louris rambled on…

"Oh, I'd like to say it was all me, but it wasn't. It was those brushes, those magical brushes. They had some kind of magical powers about them." Ader said.

The Magic Brushes

"Magical powers? Tell me more!" Louris begged.

"Yes, it all began when I was walking through an antique shop in Lanesboro. Over in the corner of the shop was an old box with some fancy baroque designs around it. Something compelled me to pick it up. The box had a rattle inside as I moved it. I turned the box over and on the bottom, there was a bible scripture. It said 1 Corinthians 13:13. I took the box over to the shopkeeper to see if he knew how to open it. I couldn't!"

Ader recalled the memory as if it were yesterday.

"Hello, my name is Ader. I am interested in buying this box. Do you know how to open it?" he asked.

"Well, it certainly looks interesting, doesn't it?" The shopkeeper said.

As the shopkeeper examined the box, he made a comment:

"This box looks like some sort of Rubik's cube." Pensive he turned the box over and over. He then pushed one end, pulled the other, gave it a turn, and pop, it opened.

"Thank you Mr." Ader said.

"Oh, my name is Harmen," he said.

"Harmen what?" he asked.

"Oh, my name is quite unusual and long. It is Harmenszoon Van Rijn. Just call me Harmen, like everyone else." He said as they both looked inside the open box.

"Well, it looks like I bought some old-time brushes." Ader said.

"It does!" The shopkeeper said. Ader placed $2.00 down on the counter, to pay for the box.

That is when Ader noticed the shopkeeper's right hand, as he took the money. His right hand had 3 very prominent dark brown moles by his thumb. Ader continued to tell his fantastic story to Louris...

"Soon I took the box out of Harmen's hand and went back home. Once there, I placed the box on top of a nightstand in my bedroom. Then, I sat down on an easy chair and stared at the box. As time passed by, the box seemed to move by itself. The movement turned into a rattle. I became terrified. Soon the box opened itself. That's when I noticed that one of the brushes was glowing. It was a bright green glow. Without hesitation, I picked up the brush that was glowing. With the brush in my hand, I started to speak. Words seemed to come right out of my mouth. Words like "I wish I could paint like the great masters. Perhaps, a great picture of my love to be." From that point on, things got a little fuzzy. I went into a very deep sleep. When I woke up, there in the middle of my bedroom floor was my easel and on the easel was a picture of a beautiful lady. It was a mystery, but not for long. At the bottom of the canvas was a name. That name was Mina Lynn. Who was this Mina Lynn? I asked myself. I had no idea."

The canvas was wet, so I placed a cloth over it until it was completely dry. Once I put away all of my art supplies, it was now time to reflect on what just happened. As I sat in my easy chair, some thoughts came into my head. I kept saying:

"Harmen, Harmen, he said his name was Harmenszoon Van Rijn. Harmenszoon Van Rijn! No! It just can't be!

Harmenszoon Van Rijn is Rembrandt. I need to go back to that antique shop now! I need to talk to Harmen. Yes, Harmen might be able to explain everything." I ran out the door of my house and headed for the shop.

As I approached the antique shop, I noticed that there was a sign in the door window that said, "Out for Lunch, back in 1 hour" So, I waited. Soon another man came up to the shop and opened the door. I spoke up.

"Say Mr., I would like to speak to Harmen."

"Harmen! There is no Harmen here." He said.

"But I was just here about an hour ago. I bought a small box from Harmen. Could I speak to him?" I asked.

"You must be mistaken. I am the only one who runs this shop. I am the owner. Sorry! You can stay and shop around if you'd like." he said. By now, I was quite confused. Was I losing my mind? I departed the shop and went home.

The very next day, I set up my easel and sat down in my easy chair. Slowly I contemplated; should I or should I not paint another picture? Would I be wasting the next brush on painting something foolish? Should I try and see what happens? I decided to use one of my own personal brushes that I stored in my easel case.

"Nothing. That's right, nothing happened. No matter how hard I tried to paint a masterpiece, the quality was just not the same as that picture of Mina."

I sat there in my chair for the longest tine, staring

at Mina's portrait. I began to wonder, was I somehow going to meet this person?

Did I have some unknown destiny with her? Maybe I should just go with it and see what happens.

Those brushes that were in the box, were endowed with great powers. It was like they were alive and ready to listen to my request. "Louris, I was a fraud. I asked that glowing brush to paint like the great master. And so, it came to be.

"Shortly after I finished painting Mina's picture, I met her. It was amazing! How does a person paint a picture of a person who he has never met or seen before, and then, three days later he meets that same person? It was magic!" Ader said to Louris.

"How can you be sure that it was magic? Perhaps it might have been destiny!" Louris said.

"Magic, Destiny, God, call it what you will. Soon I became very possessive of those three remaining brushes. I finally decided to bury one of them under a board in the woodshed behind our house at 1910 Bergen Street. I carefully wrapped one of the brushes in an oil-soaked cloth and placed it in a box. On top of the box, I laid a lucky silver dollar. Then, I buried the box. I gave you a second silver dollar years later. I hope you still have that gift." Ader said.

"Tell me more about the box, grandfather." Louris said.

"As I said earlier, I buried the box under a board in the woodshed. It is about 8 inches down covered by dirt. Years later, it burned down and then my mother planted a garden in its place. The box, where it is now, I don't know. Somewhere in that garden. One thing is for sure

Louris, I buried that box with one of those brushes and placed a lucky silver dollar on top of the box." Ader said.

"Grandfather, didn't you say that you used one brush to paint Mina? You buried one brush in the garden. Where are the other two brushes?" Louris asked Ader.

"Yes, that is what I said. Louris, I have in my possession two of the magic brushes. They are both in the bottom drawer of my dresser. Take them. I want you to have them. I only ask that you use them for something special. There will come a time in your life when you experience a defining moment. That's when you should use them." Ader said.

"I will grandfather. You have my word on that." Louris assured grandfather.

"I chose to use a brush to find the love of my life, and I did. I found Mina, your grandmother. She was the greatest treasure in this world. If you do the same, you will be glad you did. Love is the greatest gift." Ader said to Louris.

"Wow, choosing the love of his life over the wealth of this world, and then feeling glad that he did. Happiness! I want some of that!" Louris thought.

My visit with grandfather soon came to an end. I grabbed the two remaining brushes from his dresser and headed back home.

Once in my studio bedroom at home, I pushed all my art supplies over to a corner. I set up my easel and blank canvas. There, lying on top of my nightstand was one of my brushes. It was glowing. The glow pulsated. It seemed to be waiting for my instructions. What should I request? I became unsure. So, I decided not to decide. I resolved to put everything away for a later date.

Time passed and I daydreamed of the future this blessing would bring me. Often I would find myself staring, my eyes fixated on that demanding, pulsating glow.

Something. There had to be something that was so important for me to act. What was it? What was waiting out there in the world that had to be worthy of my actions? I did promise grandfather that I would use a brush for a defining moment. What was that defining moment? Maybe, just maybe, there might be something going on here that is greater than my understanding. I know, I'll just put it off until tomorrow. Louris thought.

And so, days went by. Weeks went by. Soon the summer roses became autumn leaves. During the summer, I managed to paint four pictures with my own store-bought brushes. They were very good, but not what a person would call a masterpiece.

Patiently I waited for that great defining moment so I could use one of those magic brushes, but it never came.

Soon, late fall arrived, and I was now spending most of my time at the cannery. Working at a job that I didn't like, but it was necessary to have a steady income. Painting is a great passion, but most of the time, passion does not pay the bills. My income helped our household at 1910 Bergen Street.

I was now in the winter of my 26th year. All I had was a handful of paintings and a sturdy back with short hours at work. Our fall canning at the factory had moved along at a slow pace once winter arrived. My income became less and less.

There is a lot of guilt placed upon a person when his income falls short of what is expected. I admit it. I was tempted to use one of those magic brushes to paint a great masterpiece and become a socialist Santa Claus, but I was compelled to wait for some grand moment. For now, the magic brushes were safe in the box.

All I could do was wait for spring. Spring, that is when I can set up my painting work area on the back porch.

Oh, the smell of fresh oils on the canvas. The warm sun in May. I can barely wait. Perhaps I will be blessed with a few picture sales. If not, maybe a grand masterpiece will show itself! Who knows? Life is full of surprises. One must always be ready for the unexpected.

Suddenly, grandfather's voice came into Louris's head.

"Louris, I want you to use these brushes for a grand defining moment."

"Oh, why did I make him that promise?" Louris said.

It was May. Spring was in full swing. The air was clean, dry, and smelled of grass. A great day to set up my easel on the back porch. By now, I felt that my life was going nowhere. Any self-esteem I might have had was in the wind. Life is not just about me, me, me. Shouldn't there be an us? I needed to be part of an "US." It worked for my grandfather. Why couldn't it work for me?

I couldn't put it off one more moment. I set up my easel as planned. I removed the glowing brush from the box. I stood there for the longest time in front of the canvas. I was very nervous.

The New Painting

In a soft voice, I spoke the same words that my grandfather Ader had spoken 51 years earlier:

"I wish I could paint like the great masters and paint a picture of my love to be."

I picked up the glowing brush and started to paint. To my amazement, everything started to come together. A picture of a beautiful young girl was appearing before my very eyes. Soon, I became exhausted and started to get sleepy. I laid down and went into a deep sleep. When I woke up, there it was, a finished picture of a young lady. At the bottom of the canvas was a name. The name was "Amy." Who was Amy?

I placed a white cloth over the canvas to keep the dust off of it. Then I went back into the house. On the coffee table was a newspaper. A breeze came in from the window and started to turn the pages of the newspaper. One by one they turned, and then it stopped. I looked down and there was an advertisement for an art show. It was going to be showing in three days at Phalen Park, St. Paul Minnesota. My compulsion was to go. So, I did.

It did not take too long to put up my display booth at the park. My display was not very large, but it did consist of eight of my best paintings; and then there was my new grand masterpiece, Amy. I covered it with a white cloth to keep the dust off the fresh paint.

This "Art in the Park" showing started out like a usual art show. There were many lookers, but no sales. Then all of the sudden, there she was, walking past all of the booths. Suddenly, she stopped at mine. She looked at all my art and spoke to me. "These pictures are good. Have you been painting long?" She asked.

"Oh, I have been painting for several years, but I still feel that I have more things to learn," I said.

"What is that picture over there with the white cloth over the canvas?" She asked.

"That is the one I painted most recently," I explained.

"Could I see it?" She asked.

"Sure!" I said as I removed the cloth. She just stared at the picture and looked back at me.

"Why, it is a picture of me. You painted a picture of me. I don't even know you. How did you do that?" She asked. She stared at the picture again and said, "Yes, that's me. Look, I am even wearing the same blue dress."

Just then, two men came over to Louris's booth. The older gentleman stopped at the portrait of Amy. He just stared for the longest time.

"Winslow, my eyeglass, hand me my eyeglass," the old gentleman said to his friend.

With the eyeglass, which was a magnifying glass, he scanned over the entire portrait. With a low voice he said, "My God! This is Van Rijn. This is Van Rijn."

"Van Rijn? Who is that?" Amy asked.

Winslow looked at Amy and said, "Professor Pierre Dupre refers to the artist as 'Harmenszoon Van Rijn.' The general public knows Van Rijn as 'Rembrandt.'"

"Winslow! Come over here. Look! Can you see what a grand thing this young man has done?" the older gentleman said.

211

A New Job in Monterey

"Just look at his portrayal, his use of light and shadow and all those warm colors that bring out the innermost feelings of his subject. Absolutely fantastic. Oh, Van Rijn, you have come back to us. You are here once again," the professor said repeatedly.

"Winslow, fetch this young man one of my business cards."

"Louris, did you say that your name is Louris?" the professor asked.

"Yes, my name is Louris Van Muessen," Louris said.

"Well, Mr. Van Muessen, there is a national art show in Monterey, California in four weeks. I would be greatly honored if you would come there and be my personal guest. I will provide you with housing and all the arrangements. Here is my card. I hope to see you there. Bring some of your best portraits" The professor said.

"Sir, we have to leave soon if you are going to make your appointment," Winslow said to the professor.

The professor and his friend Winslow departed the art show.

Louris pulled out the professor's business card and read the first line across the face of the card. It read: Professor Pierre Dupre, Curator, Louvre Paris Museum.

"Wow! That is quite impressive. I think you should go to Monterey and display some of your pictures," Amy said.

"So, Amy, are you a fan of art?" Louris asked.

"Your art! I think I would like to see more of you – your art, that is," Amy said.

They both laughed. It did not take very long. Louris and Amy soon found themselves spending a great deal of time with each other.

Louris always felt uncomfortable picking up Amy at the back door of her Summit Avenue estate on Summit Hill in St. Paul; but she had her reasons. Her father was an overbearing and judgmental character from an older generation. To put it plain and direct, he didn't like anybody who wasn't wealthy, and Amy knew it.

One Saturday while her father Derry was out of town, Amy snuck out the back door and met Louris. They both went to Lake Phalen in St. Paul and had a picnic. As they were laying on the blanket and looking at the sky, Amy asked Louris, "Of all the places in the world, where would you like to be?"

Louris replied, "Somewhere on a beach in the South of France. Nice. Yes, Nice, France. That is where I would like to visit. But not alone, with you!" Louris replied.

"Maybe someday that will happen. It will be us. Just the two of us – forever." Amy said.

"I would like that very much. I will always want and need your love." They kissed.

When their picnic was over, Louris took Amy home. Once again, it was through the back door. Amy ran right through the back door and right into her father, who had come back from his trip early.

"And so.. Why in the world are you flying through the house so fast these days? Is there something I should know?" Derry asked.

Amy looked down and squinted her eyes for a second and blurted out, "I have a boyfriend."

"A boyfriend? And what is this boyfriend's name?" Derry asked.

"Louris, his name is Louris Van Muessen."

"And what does this boyfriend do for a living? He does work, doesn't he?" Derry remarked.

"He is an artist. Someday he is going to be a very famous artist," Amy said.

"I see... so he is going to be a famous artist who sneaks about homes and stops at the back door, is he?" Derry said in a sarcastic tone.

"I knew you wouldn't understand. You never understand anything unless it is something that pleases you." Amy stormed off and ran up the stairway to her room. Allison, Amy's mother then came into the room.

"What is going on here, Derry?" She asked.

"Your daughter is sneaking about town to be with some good-for-nothing, unemployed wannabe artist. It is time to put an end to this nonsense. An artist! Ha, I bet you he plays with finger paints. My daughter can do better than that!" Derry said with more sarcasm.

"Have you ever met this Louris?" Allison asked Derry.

"No but it's all the same as I said!" Derry shouted.

Derry Meets Louris

"I think you should meet this young man. I am going to go upstairs and talk to your daughter," Allison said.

"Fine, you do that!" Derry said. After about 15 minutes in passing, Allison came back downstairs.

"It is all settled. Tomorrow night, which is Sunday night, Louris is coming over here. We will meet him then," Allison said.

"Fine, once and for all we will get things back to normal," Derry said.

Sunday night came quickly. This time Louris was at the front door. Lena Flynn, the maid, let him in. And there they were – Allison, Derry, Amy and Louris all standing in the doorway of Amy's Summit Avenue house.

"Come in, please come into our home." Allison said. Amy started in with the introductions.

"And so, Mr. Van Muessen, whereabouts does the rest of your family reside? Where are you from?" Allison asked.

"Oh, I am from a small town in southeastern Minnesota called Lanesboro," Louris said.

"So, what brings you way up here in the cities?" Derry asked.

"It was the art show in Phalen Park in St. Paul. I set up an art booth there."

"So how do you make a real living?" Derry asked with a sarcastic tone.

"Derry! Stop that," Allison spoke up. Amy hurried the formal conversation to an abrupt end.

"Louris, we are going to have to leave soon if we are going to make that movie."

She knew where the conversation was heading. She knew what the next question was going to be: Are you Catholic? Amy quickly nudged Louris out the door and soon they were gone.

"Did you see the look on his face when I asked him if he had a real job? I don't like him. He has squinty untrustworthy eyes. Oh, I have always regretted that this day would come. My own daughter, my own flesh and blood, dating an artist bum. I tell ya, this world is surely coming to an end. I was fearful that one day my daughter might show up at our front door with some atheist motorcycle vagrant, who was unemployed with no prospects. She shows up at our doorstep with some unemployed wannabe artist and I'll bet that he is Protestant besides. I tell you; life is not going to be kind to me now unless I put a stop to this nonsense," Derry said.

"Stop yourself, right now. You are talking crazy," Allison said.

"Stop yourself you say? Did you not see those beady eyes? His eyes are devious. Surely those eyes are not smiling," Derry said.

"What face were you looking at? Was it yours? I saw a fine young gentleman. Now that we are talking about faces, you didn't shave today. Why don't you go back in the bathroom and look into the mirror? Hopefully, you will see an adult for once," Allison admonished Derry.

Derry was rubbing the right side of his face as he walked away from Allison.

Several days later, Derry was in his home library when he heard the house phone ring. Amy ran right over to the phone and picked up the receiver.

The Phone Call

Derry moved close to the living room doorway and listened to Amy's conversation.

"You didn't! You are actually going all the way out to Monterey, California to enter some of your paintings into that art festival contest? So how long are you going to be there? That contest is not going to be until June 28. What? You might stay there and look for a job! But I'll miss you. I don't think I could do that. My father would be very angry. We can't live together!" Amy said.

Derry's eyes were almost popping out of their sockets. He quietly backed away from the doorway.

That evening at the supper table, Derry announced he had to travel to Pittsburgh on the weekend of the 28th of June. That he had some business at one of the steel plants that he owned, and it was necessary for him to be there.

"So, how long are you going to be there?" Allison asked.

"Oh, as long as it takes to get some real business done, once and for all." Derry said.

Soon, the 28th of June came, and Derry was off to make his business deal. He stopped by his friend Sean's place and picked him up. They both went to the airport and purchased a round trip ticket for Monterey, California.

Once there in Monterey, Sean rented a car, and they made their way over to the art festival. Sean located

Louris's booth at the festival and pointed him out to Derry.

"You wait right here, Sean. I'll have a few private words with Mr. Louris Van Muessen," Derry said.

The Bribe

Derry approached Louris. Both of them locked eyes on each other.

"Skip the formalities; I'll make this quite clear. I don't like you. In fact, I never want to see your shadow darken our doorstep again. Here is $50,000. Make sure that what I say happens. Never again!" Derry stuffed the envelope into Louris's shirt pocket and departed.

"Sean, now that we got the car, let's take a little drive down the coast to L.A. I think that the horses are running at Hollywood Turf Park. Maybe we can make it there before the second race. Owen Brinkman will be there. He is one of my accountants. He always sits in the same spot. He will be easy to find. Let's go!" Derry spoke with a positive voice.

Sean and Derry found Owen at the seating area that he always sat at. Derry made some side bets with Owen on the horses. Derry always bet on a horse whose owner had an Irish last name. If that didn't work, he would bet on a horse whose jockey was wearing green.

Owen cleaned up on all his side bets with Derry. He beat Derry seven out of seven horse races. It was a bad day at the track for Derry. Derry left the track about $12,000 less than was planned for.

As soon as Derry arrived at home, his wife Allison greeted him at the door.

"So how did your trip to Pittsburgh go for you?" She asked.

"Oh, everything is going to be okay, now that I cleared up the mess," Derry said.

"Good, I'm glad that everything got straightened out. You are a man that gets things done," Allison said.

Straightened out, she said. Get things done, she says. I hope that she is right, Derry thought.

As Derry sat in his favorite easy chair, he started to think about Amy and Louris. That's when the phone rang. Lena, the housekeeper answered it. It was Louris and he wanted to talk to Amy. Soon as the days went by, this became a usual event. Every time it happened, Derry became more and more concerned.

"Lena, could you please come into my study? I would like to have a word with you," Derry requested. Derry walked into his study and closed the door behind Lena.

"Okay, I want you to listen to what I am about to say. Amy is not to be speaking on the phone with that good-for-nothing Louris Van Muessen. Do I make myself clear? If he ever calls here again, just tell him Amy is indisposed and is with another gentleman. Is that understood?" Derry demanded.

"Yes, Mr. O'Konner," Lena answered.

It was about 3 more days of phone calls from Louris and then they stopped all together. That is when the letters started to arrive for Amy. Once again, Derry took control of the situation. He told Lena when she picked up the daily mail, any letter from Louris was to be given to him. That was his new order for Lena. She complied.

One day as Derry sat in his library study, the whole situation seemed to be out of control. He had tried plan

"A." That was to bribe Louris, but money didn't seem to work. Louris was in Derry's eyes, a threat. Things were about to escalate. Derry picked up his phone and made a call.

"Seanie boy, are you busy? Well just forget about that for now. Stop what you are doing. Listen up. If Louris gets a good job in Monterey, I'll lose Amy. She'll start living with him. Here is what I want you to do. Be ready to go to Monterey at any time when I call you. I'll make it well worth your while." Derry said.

Two weeks later, Derry made his call to Sean.

"Seanie boy, I think I got some work for you. I found out that Louris is working as an understudy for Mr. Pierre DuPre at a museum in Monterey. I want you to go there and grab some artifacts and hide them real good. Put them in their basement or whatever – just hide them. Louris will get blamed for their disappearance. They will think he is a thief; then he will lose his job. Then Amy will not leave here to be with an unemployed bum. It will work for certain. I am sure of it," Derry said.

"When you said that you would make it worth my while, what does that really mean?" Sean asked.

"A new car. You have been talking about new cars. Let's make it one that you would really like driving. Just get this job done," Derry demanded.

"Okay, I'll be leaving tomorrow morning," Sean said.

Soon everything came to be. Sean stole the artifacts, Louris got fired. The newspapers said that a quarter of a million dollars was stolen at the museum.

Louris on the Run

Everything was now out of control. Sean made a desperate call to Derry.

"Say, Derry, this is Sean. Can I talk freely?"

"Yes, go ahead," Derry said.

"You know that new car that I was talking about? Well, scratch that! I was thinking I would like to have a truck, a good sized one. One that could pull a 30-foot camper." Sean said.

"What? Our deal was for a car," Derry said.

"Yeah, that was before I learned the price of the artifacts." Sean said. There was a long silence.

"Okay, come back home. Your job is done," Derry said as he hung up the phone. Derry stood there in his home library and smiled and whispered in a low voice, "Everything is going to be normal again." But was it?

Louris went back to Lanesboro and to his rented studio apartment. That evening he tossed and turned and had a terrible time falling asleep. Finally in the morning, he went over to the bathroom to shave his face. As he stood looking into the mirror, he started to have a conversation with himself.

"Amy, what should I do about Amy? I can't give her a life of hiding from the police. She deserves better than that! Maybe I should just leave and never come back. She will find someone else to fall in love with. I am sure of that; she is such a great catch. And then there are my parents. Even though they live in another state,

223

I can't go back there. By now the police have already been to their house to check for my presence. Oh, I hope they don't think they raised a son who became a thief wanted by the law.

Oh, God, why is this all happening to me? Why? Why? Lord, can you please help me?" Louris said while he paused to look into his own eyes as he was shaving his face.

After Louris finished shaving his face, he went back to his bed and flopped down and stared at the ceiling. All the while, he laid there and tried to make an emergency plan for his life. He eventually got up, looked out his apartment window. There on the street below was a deputy sheriff's car that had pulled up to his apartment. The deputy stepped out of his car and went across the street to another building. Suddenly another sheriff's car pulled up outside.

The deputy sheriff came out of the building across the street. Without hesitation, he walked over to the sheriff's car that had just arrived.

"Say Leon, I just talked to a person living in the apartment across the street. He said the car parked out front belongs to someone with Louris Van Muessen's description. Why don't I run that license plate? That will tell us what we need to know," the deputy said.

Meanwhile Louris was looking at the impending arrest that was soon coming. He slowly moved his apartment curtain back in place. He had seen enough. Quickly, Louris made his escape plan and moved into action; for time was running out. Without hesitation, Louris stuffed $100 into an envelope with a brief note stating "Thank you Lyle, for being patient with the rent balance. I'll be gone for a few days. I am going to the Rochester airport." Louris placed the envelope on the tabletop next to a couple of half-filled coffee cups that he had just warmed up in the microwave oven. Swiftly, he unlocked his apartment door and crawled under his bed. Concealing himself with a large bedspread over the top of his bed.

Within a couple of minutes, both the sheriff and the deputy came into his room. The sheriff went over to the table and opened the letter. He read the letter and said to the deputy as he placed his hands over the two cups of coffee. "Great, now Louris has got some help with his escape."

"What do you mean? How do you know that?" The deputy asked.

"Well, both these cups are still warm. That means he couldn't be gone for more than 10 minutes. We need to get to the Rochester airport now! Let's go!" The sheriff said as he rushed out of the apartment.

Once the deputy and the sheriff left Louris's apartment, Louris came out from under his bed. He then walked over to his window and pulled his curtain to the side a little bit. Looking down, he witnessed both the deputy and the sheriff speeding off towards Rochester.

Louris stepped back away from the window. Looking to his side, he noticed that one of his magic brushes was glowing.

"That's it!" He shouted. Quickly, Louris assembled his painting tools and began painting. It was a beach scene. It was a picture of a person walking on the beach with the sunset at his back. The person was, of course,

Louris. He named the painting, "Sunset Beach in Nice France."

After walking up after his sleep – there he was, on the beach. Right where he always wanted to be.

Tested Faith

And so, it came to be, here was Louris, hiding out in a foreign land; thanks to the efforts of Derry O'Konner.

In desperation, Louris set up a small art stand on the beach in Nice France. The time had come where he had no outside support. He resorted to do what he knew best: paint pictures for sale.

Wherever Louris set up his stand on the beach, he always brought along his most treasured picture of Amy – the love of his life. To protect her painting, he covered the canvas with a white cloth, so the sun would not fade her image.

One special summer day, Louris set up his paint stand the same as all the other days, but today something very special was about to happen. A man was walking towards him using a walking stick. It took him a long time to reach Louris, but their eyes eventually met.

"So, how are sales today Louris?" the man said with a smile.

"Sir, do I know you? Louris responded.

"Oh, I have heard your name mentioned several times. You know Louris, around here, you have a good reputation as an artist." The man said.

"That's good! I'd rather have friends than enemies." Louris responded.

"I see you take very good care of that picture over there, under the white towel. May I see it?" The man asked.

"You may." Louris said. The old man removed the towel and picked up the picture and stared at Amy's portrait.

"I see you have a fantastic ability and through light you have captured the charm and passion of this beautiful woman. What would you say if I offered you $100,000 for this portrait?" The man asked.

"I'd have to say no! This is Amy, the love of my life." Louris said.

"I see! She must mean a great deal to you." The man responded.

"What a coincidence! Look who is coming down the beach. It is Remi Martin. He is a very wealthy collector of fine arts. Remi always gets what he wants because of his enormous wealth. Let's see how far he is willing to go for the price of your painting. I will out-bid him and let's both see what happens." The man said.

The man held up the painting with both hands and stared at the painting. Louris noticed three distinct moles near his right-hand thumb. He recognized the hand, but where? Where in my past was there such a hand? Louris thought.

"Louris, I'll give you two hundred thousand dollars for your painting," The man said.

This got Remi's attention. He walked over to the painting and stared at it with delight.

"Fantastic, simply fantastic!" Remi said as he placed the painting back on the easel.

Meanwhile, the old man went over to the wet sand on the beach and wrote in the sand two words with his walking stick. The words were "Pertemto Fidem."

He turned around and walked back to Louris and said, "I'll give you $500,000 for your painting."

Louris simply said, "No thank you."

Remi took the bait. He pulled out a monocle and examined the picture.

"I'll give you one million dollars for the picture. What do you say?" Remi asked.

By now, the bidding war was in full swing.

"I'll give you three million for the picture." The man said.

"Enough, enough of this waste of my time. I have no time for this haggling, ten million dollars and that's my final offer" Remi said.

"Sorry, no sale." Louris said.

Remi threw his hands up and walked away in disgust.

"Louris, you know that I could have gotten up to twenty million dollars for the picture. Oh, if I just had five more minutes!" The old man said as he too started to walk away.

Louris walked over to the wet sand on the beach and read the two words in a low voice. He said, "Pertemto Fidem."

As he turned around to call back the old man, the water washed up onto the beach and washed away the words.

"Come back, come back." Louris yelled for a response from the man, but he was now too far away.

Louris knew the saying and its meaning. Pertemto Fidem is old Latin for: "Test of Faith."

"Keep up your good faith, Louris and thank the good Lord that you are not rich or poor. Everything is going to work out for the good Louris! Goodness and grace will follow you all the days of your life." The man yelled back.

"Thank the good Lord that you are not rich or poor!" the man said.

"Why, that is what my mother said at our suppertime prayers." Louris said to himself.

Louris looked towards the man in the distance and yelled "Come back, come back so we can talk for a while!" Louris requested.

"I can't! I have to go see my friend Raphael." The man said. In an instant he disappeared. The man vanished.

That evening back on Summit Hill where Amy lived, everyone had a quiet supper. There seemed to be very little to talk about. So, after supper, everyone went about their business.

Lena, the housemaid, approached Mr. O'Konner in his library study and presented him with a package that had arrived earlier in the day.

"Mr. O'Konner, I kept this package in the closet. It is addressed to you, so here it is," Lena said.

"Thanks, Lena. Thank you for being so discrete." Derry took the package and placed it on his desktop. Lena quickly departed.

Once Lena was gone, Derry opened the package and saw it was the very same envelope that he had given Louris. It appeared to be unopened. Quickly, Derry looked around the room and found a place to hide his envelope, or was it his shame?

Angry Allison

His shame was now hidden behind some books on a library shelf.

The following day was going to be just a normal day, or was it? Allison was pacing back and forth throughout the house, slamming doors, and swearing. Her anger seemed to be directed at Derry, but he wasn't even home yet. Finally, she heard him come through the front door. Derry walked into his library and opened some of his mail, and then sat down in his reading chair. He opened a book that he had almost finished and then in came an angry Allison.

With her loud voice, she yelled out with slow words, "What...did...you...do?"

"I almost read this entire book!" was his response.

"You know what I mean," Allison said. At that very moment Amy was coming down the stairs from her room. She stopped and listened to Allison's loud voice. She began eavesdropping.

"I have just had a long talk with Lena. You remember Sean's sister. Aren't you just a little bit interested in what she has told me?" Allison yelled out.

"No! I don't usually make time to listen to gossip," Derry responded.

"Well, you better make time today. It seems that her brother Sean has had a little too much brandy to drink. When Sean drinks, he likes to talk and that is what he did in front of Lena. According to Sean, he went out to Monterey, California and his friend gave Louris an envelope that had $50,000 in it. And guess what his friend demanded that Louris should never do again?

He demanded that Louris should never see our daughter Amy again. Oh, and it gets even better. Guess who this low-life friend of Sean's is?" Allison asked.

"Now, now, Allison, you should not listen to idle gossip. Especially coming from the likes of Sean Flynn. He is a known storyteller. He likes to tell tall tales. You know the type!" Derry said.

"Oh! Can you just stop yourself? Stop lying. Isn't it enough that you gave him a bribe? Now you have gotten him in trouble with the law," Allison said.

"Flynn, that lying Flynn. He will say anything. He can't be trusted," Derry said muttering to himself.

"How could you be so horrible?" Allison asked. "Do you know what else he told Lena?" Allison asked.

"No! It is like I said before. I don't listen to idle talk," Derry said with assurance.

"Well, clean out your ears. I have more bad news. Sean told Lena that your so-called business trip took you all the way down to L.A. and to Hollywood turf horse racing track, where you lost a small fortune of $12,000. What is this thing that you have with Louris? Why are you so against him? He seems like a very nice gentleman. He is fine for our daughter Amy. They make a wonderful couple. Why?" Allison asked.

"I don't like him. He is a beady-eyed bum. Eyes that you cannot trust. Besides, he is a Protestant. You know the type and he is not one of us," Derry said.

"Not one of us? Allison asked.

"You know!" Derry paused in silence. "He's not wealthy or Catholic and he is not Irish! There, I said it.

He is not Irish! I'll say it again. He is not Irish!" Derry said.

"Do you know how crazy you sound? Let me get this straight. You lied multiple times. You went to Monterey to make your bribe. Then, you went to L.A. to play the horses with Sean. And then there is Owen Brinkman! That doesn't sound very Irish to me, now does it. It sounds rather German, wouldn't you say? I always thought that you had only Irish friends!" Allison said with a sarcastic tone.

"Oh, now Allison, That's not the same. That was business. Brinkman is one of my accountants. He likes to play the horses. We share that love of horses together," Derry said.

"Will you just stop yourself? Do you even know what a hypocrite you sound like? Can't you see what a negative effect you have on other people, especially our daughter? How would you like to be on the receiving end of all your crap? Just think about all the stress you have created. You need to be less indifferent and more inclusive," Allison said.

"More inclusive! What do you mean by that?" Derry asked.

"Stop thinking of ways to push reasonable people away. Just look at all the pain that you have caused our daughter Amy. She was in love with Louris, and you did everything you could to separate them. You punished him for loving our Amy. What were you thinking? Or were you thinking?

This whole thing was not about you, you, you. If you can't see that, then we don't belong together," Allison said.

"Yes, dear, I'll try that and see what happens," Derry said.

By now, Amy heard enough. She ran upstairs to her room and began to cry.

"So, I suppose it is just business when I have to listen to our daughter cry her eyes out every night because some stupid insensitive thing that you have done," Allison said.

"Now, Allison, I will make it right. I'll bring him back. Don't worry. Things will turn out Okay, you'll see," Derry said.

That evening at supper, Derry apologized to Amy. Amy was unresponsive.

"He actually took that money. He took that money!" Amy repeated herself.

"Yes, dear, he did. But he brought it all back." Derry said.

"But now he is gone. I'll never find him," Amy said.

"Don't worry, we will all find a way!" Derry said with a reassuring smile.

Days went by. Weeks went by. Everyday Amy would run down to the bottom of the stairs and ask Lena, the housekeeper, if there was a letter for her from Louris. Her answer was always the same, no.

One day, Amy just laid in her bed and stared at the ceiling. She began to ponder.

"What would Louris have done? Where would he go? Then, it all became quite clear.

Amy Unites with Louris

He must have gone to his favorite place in the whole world. Yes! He must have gone to Nice, France. That was his favorite place, on his bucket list of places to see. Amy was not about to give up on her soul mate.

"The magic brush. I need to find that magic brush he left in the garden behind his boyhood cottage. Yes! That is what I need to do," Amy thought.

That night, Amy approached Derry in his library.

"Papa, could you please buy me a metal detector?" Amy asked.

"What on earth for? Derry said.

"Please just do it!" Amy requested.

Two days later, Derry bought Amy her request.

The next day, there she was. Amy was using the metal detector to search behind Louris's boyhood home in Lanesboro, Minnesota. She remembered the garden and began her search there. The entire property now was abandoned.

Amy searched the entire day and found nothing, but that wasn't going to stop her. As sure as the sun came up the next day, there she was, searching her heart out. Then, suddenly the metal detector started to click. With a garden hand shovel, she started to remove dirt as fast as she could. With anticipation, her hand shovel hit something solid. It was metal. She cleared away a little dirt and stood up and stared down at the bottom of the hole. It was a shiny silver dollar.

This was no ordinary silver dollar. It was a silver dollar with a nick on it. It was Ader's lucky silver dollar. Amy knew about the box and the silver dollar that was hidden years earlier.

Beneath the silver dollar was a box. Amy brushed away the dirt on the box and then opened it. Inside, was an old painting brush. Not an ordinary brush. This one glowed. It was Ader's.

Amy grabbed the box and the coin and returned to her home on Summit Hill. Once there, she went straight up to her bedroom. In her closet were some paint supplies. She pulled out all her supplies and grabbed the glowing brush and started to paint a picture. It was a picture of a woman and man on a foreign beach far away, with the sunset in the background.

Amy went over to her desk and wrote a note to her mother Allison. It briefly said: "Mom, everything is Okay. I went to be with the love of my life, Louris!"

Several hours later, Allison came home. She started to call out for Amy, but there was no answer. Allison went up to her room. On Amy's desk there was a note. Allison opened the note and read some unexpected words. By now, Allison was stunned. She looked all around the room and there in the middle of the room was just a painting, but where was Amy? She was where she wanted to be, in Nice France on the beach with Louris.

Allison had no idea of what had just happened in Amy's bedroom. It would be about eight months later when she would find out all the answers to her questions.

Little did Allison know about how Amy had painted herself into the life of Louris. Once the painting was completed, she fell asleep and woke up on the beach. Amy began walking towards a figure several hundred feet away.

There was no response from him until Amy flipped the lucky coin into the air and said these words: "Louris, I found Ader's lucky coin!"

The coin landed in the sand with the nick at the top. Sure enough, Louris concluded that this truly was his lucky coin.

Instantly the young woman raised the brim of her San Diego sun hat, to reveal her smiling face. It was Amy. The love of his life. They both embraced and sealed it with a kiss as they walked towards the sunset.

About eight months later, Louris and Amy made their way back to Summit Hill and her parent's estate house. When they arrived, Derry and Allison were standing in the garden.

"I can't figure out where that girl has gone. Even the police can't figure it out. I wonder if that good-for-nothing herring chocker Louris has done something bad to our poor Amy. Oh, if I could just get my hands around his throat, I would give him what he deserves," Derry said.

The clouds were coming in for a light rain shower. There they both were. It was Amy and Louris walking straight towards Allison and Derry, who were in the garden.

"Oh, thank you Lord. With your clouds you have decided to bless us with some joyous sunshine. You have given us back our Amy," Derry said. Tears of joy were flowing down their faces.

Once Amy and Louris approached them both in the garden, Allison made the comment, "It looks like you are carrying a child."

The Homecoming

"That is true!" Amy said, after hugging her mother Allison said.

"I hope you both can stay. We will set up a room for you both," Allison said.

"I suppose you know by now, Louris is wanted by the law. Staying here would be out of the question. Louris and I lasted in France as long as we could, but he sold all of his paintings except for one. A man offered him $10,000,000 for it, but he said no," Amy said.

"Why didn't you take the money?" Allison asked.

"It was a picture of me! He just said no," Amy said.

Derry was doing a slow burn inside. He waited for a few minutes and then, when Louris walked Amy over to a garden chair, he whispered to Allison, "Did you see that? He didn't even put a ring on her finger. That low life!" Derry said.

"Stop it right now!" Allison said.

Allison went over to Amy, who was sitting in the garden chair. Allison and Amy began to talk about the upcoming baby. After a few minutes, Allison walked back to Derry.

"So, I guess you would like to punish that evil Louris for loving our daughter?" Allison said to Derry.

"Well, before you start to punish Louris, there is something else you need to hear. Here are some interesting facts," Allison said to Derry.

"What interesting facts?" Derry asked.

"I suppose you don't know that Louris, the evil person that he is, suggested that the baby's name should be 'Derry' if it is a boy and 'Rose' if it is a girl," Allison said.

"Rose! That was my mother's name," Derry said. At this point, Derry hung his head in shame. Louris heard most of Allison's scolding of Derry. He just looked straight ahead into the garden.

After a short while, Louris got up and approached Derry and Allison and asked them if he could use their bathroom. With their permission, he started to walk towards the house. He got about 25 feet when Allison looked at Derry and said, "You have got to apologize to Louris for all your bad behavior. This was your mess. You need to make things right and I mean everything! It's time for you to own up to your shame." Allison said.

Allison's head nodded towards Louris.

"Now!" She said to Derry.

"I guess I might have been a little too overbearing. I'll tell you what, Allison dear. I will have a little talk with the lad. Nobody can ever say that Derry O'Konner, the honest man that I am, cannot correct an honest mistake," Derry said.

Derry caught up to Louris as he was walking towards the house. Suddenly Derry placed his right hand on the backside of Louris's shoulder and they continued to walk.

With his loud voice, Derry began to say, "You know, Louris, I always knew I would like you. You have got such an honest and forgiving, smiling eyes. It is a grand thing that you are doing, being that you are in such a forgiving way. Just knowing that you can forgive an old man in his misguided ways, makes me feel very proud of you. Say Louris, you must have some Irish in you. You know Louris, the good Lord loves the Irish!" Derry said.

"Oh papa, you always say that." Amy yelled out.

"Suddenly, a ray of sun broke through the clouds. It shined on the garden as Louris, and Derry stood there.

Allison looked up at the sun breaking through the clouds and said,

"Thank you, Lord. 'Tis a grand thing you have just done, Lord. You have truly blessed us all. Say, Lord… Is there any chance that you are Irish?"

The End

Acknowledgements

I want to thank my illustrator Tim Blough for creating the covers for Farris Hamley and Van Muessen and thank Erin Hongerholt for assisting me with the process of creating the concept for the artwork.

I want to thank my daughters: Kerri, Kristi, and Bonni for assisting in typing, formatting, and editing these stories.

And I want to thank my wife Sherri for her support.

Printed in the United States
by Baker & Taylor Publisher Services